2 o'clock pm
table another
tablet

Jeffrey Bernard is *still* unwell

*to
charlie
hurt*

The author caught loitering by brother Bruce

Jeffrey Bernard is *still* unwell

illustrated by
michael heath

fourth estate
london

First published in *Talking Horses* in 1987 by
Fourth Estate Limited
289 Westbourne Grove
London W11 2QA

First published in paperback in 1991
Reprinted 1991

A catalogue record for this book is available from the British Library.

ISBN 1–85702–005–7

The author and publishers would like to thank the *Spectator* and the *Sporting
Life* for permission to use material that originally appeared in their columns.

Typeset in Palatino by York House Typographic Ltd, London
Printed and bound in Great Britain by
Biddles Ltd, Guildford and King's Lynn

foreword

WHEN I WAS ABOUT SIXTEEN AND DOING TIME AT A DISGUSTING naval college called Pangbourne, a boy called Vickers was given twelve strokes of the cane – the maximum – for running a book. I was deeply impressed. That put gambling in the same wicked league as drinking and sex, and if it was that bad then I wanted some of it. So I started to read the racing pages in the Saturday papers and pretty soon I too was laying a few bets.

It didn't take long to get me hooked. Once you've risked about ten times more than you can afford and savoured the flow of adrenalin it's hard to get excited about anything else. Even my passion for my mother faded into the background. She looked like a cross between Maria Callas and Ava Gardner and I fancied her so much it nearly drove me bonkers. This new obsession with horseracing didn't exactly further the career she had planned for me as an Officer and Gentleman, though. I fell at the first by getting chucked out of the Outward Bound course designed for future high-fliers in the Blue Funnel line, and went straight to Soho to become a layabout.

I got jobs navvying and dishwashing and, believe it or not, boxing. I had been quite handy at school so I used to go down to Jack Solomon's gym and spar with 'The Aldgate Tiger', British and European Featherweight Champion Al Phillips. Rather than cash in hand my reward was a visit to the café next door. One day, Phillips gave me concussion, then Solomon took me to the café for a cup of coffee, a cheese roll and a cigarette. I was once greedy enough to climb into the ring with one of the greatest of all featherweights, Sandy Saddler, for eight quid a round, the equivalent of two weeks' wages. I didn't know what I was doing for the next three days.

Anyway, hanging around Soho wondering what to do with myself I kept being assailed by this brilliant idea of having a bet on a horse. The first time this brainwave came to me I borrowed five shillings, picked two of Manny Mercer's mounts – since I was always overhearing pub talk about what a genius the man was – and did them both in a double. You never forget the names of your first two winners: Burnt Grass and Cherry Heering. The bookmaker paid me in an alley, which made it all the more wicked, and I was almost rich. Thirty-seven years later, the struggle goes on.

Another day some years later I was sitting in the pub doing bugger all – I was supposed to be working as a stage hand – when a bookmaker friend of mine walked in and told me *The Sporting Life* were advertising for a columnist. For want of anything better to do I applied, and to my astonishment I was hired. My brief was to privide half a page twice a week, on Wednesdays and Saturdays. This was the early seventies, but I thought my wage of fifty quid was a bit of an insult, even for a stage hand. I started work the day Nijinsky came second in Le Prix de l'Arc de Triomphe.

I didn't waste words pretending I knew much about horses or waxing lyrical about such and such a trainer as if I'd known him since the cradle. I wrote about what horseracing meant to me and just about everyone else: losing money. I described all the traps and pitfalls of punting and how I fell into them with tedious regularity, and I took the piss out of the racing Establishment. The readers lapped it up. Odd things used to happen to me on 'The Life'. One night I woke up in a field outside Pontefract and I still have no idea how I got there. Another time I remember opening my eyes to find myself in bed with Barry Brogan – a great jockey, it is true, but not my idea of a desirable bed companion. And I once spent the night with a girl in the ditch of the celebrated Pond Fence at Sandown. I don't know how we met or what was so enticing about the Pond Fence – perhaps I was pointing out to her that obstacle's peculiar hazards. Anyway, we got on famously.

Exactly a year after I started this job I was sacked. There was a National Hunt dinner at a hotel in Kensington, to which I was invited as guest of honour to present an award to the woman point-to-point rider of the year. I had to give a speech – something I'd never done before – and I was nervous as hell. I went to *The Sporting Life* at the crack of dawn to start work on it. Smithfield Market was open, and I thought that if I had a couple of drinks to get me going I'd probably write rather a good one. I drank steadily from six in the morning to seven in the evening, at which time I arrived at the hotel and immediately passed out. Two waiters had to carry me upstairs and put me to bed. The next day I flew to Paris for the Arc de Triomphe. I'd been so pissed I couldn't remember anything at all. Henry Cecil walked up to me in the paddock at Longchamp and said, 'Hello, Jeffrey, what a pity you've been sacked.' It was the first I'd heard of it, but anyway, that was that. Except that I put my whole week's wages on Mill Reef and won what for me was quite a tidy sum.

This wasn't quite the end of my career as a racing journalist. Richard Ingrams dreamed up the idea of having a racing column in *Private Eye* and asked me to do it under the pseudonym 'Colonel Mad'. They were great people to work for because they let me say anthing I wanted and I had a good time taking the Mickey out of all the intolerably pompous people I'd met since I first got obsessed with horses. Of course racing people loved it. They are mostly lunatics and nutcases who live in a world of their own, can only talk about what some wretched three-year-old did yesterday or might do tomorrow, have never been to the theatre or read a book, and can't tell a Chippendale chair from a kitchen stool. What was strange was that even readers who knew nothing about racing became intrigued by the barmy people I was writing about.

Needless to say I lost this job, too. Lord Gnome began to disapprove of me. It didn't improve matters when I was interviewed once and the reporter had the rare gall to actually print what I said. He asked me why I'd fallen into disfavour with his Lordship and I told him: 'I fuck, I drink and I back horses. Not only does he do none of these things, but he can't.' Nigel Dempster took over the column and they called him 'Colonel Bonkers'. But there was a snag: Dempster isn't funny.

This brief account of my career is to give you some insight into why this is such an exceptional book. And I mean *exceptional*. Most books about racing are terrible hack jobs by jumped up sub-editors who can't write. The rest are dreary rags-to-riches 'autobiographies' about some hard-done-by apprentice who starts life in a rat-infested loft in Newmarket but by sheer talent and force of character becomes a champion jockey, and gets his just reward on his retirement when the Queen summons him to Buckingham Palace and presents him with a silver cigarette box. A famous jockey once asked me to ghost his life story. It would have been a very boring job without much money in it, but I said I'd do it if he owned up. He stared at me as if I'd gone mad. 'What do you mean, own up?' I told him there'd be no point in trotting out another achingly dull racing book unless he spilt the beans about the horses he'd pulled, the owners he'd conned – explained, in fact, exactly what a devious bastard he was. By this time he knew I was in urgent need of psychiatric attention. 'I'd get my badge taken away . . . I'd be warned off . . . I could never show my face in Lambourn again . . . ' he spluttered. I told him in that case I wasn't interested.

Of course there are exceptions – for instance, *Men and Horses I Have Known* by George Lambton, Jack Leach's *Sods I Have Cut on the Turf* and best of all, *The History of the Derby Stakes* by Roger Mortimer, one of the funniest raconteurs in the business. And not every racing journalist is a hack. Richard Baerlein is not only a serious punter but a good writer, too; and Charles Benson and Clive Graham, both of whom were 'The Scout' on the *Daily Express*, were always worth reading.

Come to think of it, men like these have forgotten more about racing than I will ever know. Who hasn't?

1

I ONCE WENT TO AN EVENING MEETING AT WINDSOR, GOT absolutely pissed, lost every penny in my pocket, and had no idea how to get back to London after the last. I was almost the final person to leave the racecourse and, standing desolately in the car-park, I suddenly saw a beautiful white Rolls Royce slowly approaching. I stood in its way and signalled to it to stop. It stopped. The owner, as suave as a film-star, asked what he could do for me. I said, 'I'm pissed and potless. Will you please take me to the Dorchester immediately and buy me a drink.' I'd never seen him before and I've never seen him since, but he was absolutely charming. He recognised someone who'd done their bollocks and was feeling thirsty. He drove me straight to the American Bar and stood me a huge one. We never introduced ourselves. He just filled me up and then gave me the taxi fare to get back to Soho.

That is typical of what happens at the races. You wouldn't find it at a football game or a cricket match. The racing world is stuffed with lunatics, criminals, idiots, charmers, bastards and exceptionally nice people. When you're on form and don't mind losing a few notes, a day at the races is one of the most magical days you can imagine, and the lure of the ever-changing racing circus soon becomes irresistible. What follows is a loosely chronological description of my shambling progress through a racing year, with plenty of red herrings and tangents. It runs from about August 1976 to September 1977 because I happen to have that year documented. But it could be any year, last year, next year. Except that you get a different bunch of horses to bankrupt yourself on.

On the first Saturday in August I decided Newmarket was good enough for me. The crowds at Goodwood, and at Royal Ascot come to that, always put me off attending these classier meetings. The Sloane Square mob get in the way of the racing and there are just too many people who go to be seen and who aren't really at the races at all. So I picked Newmarket, and got there early enough to go up to the gallops with Bill Marshall.

I watched him go up the new gallop on Long Hill sitting tight on an old enemy of mine, Peranka. On the Tuesday before, that horse had run pretty well enough in the Stewards' Cup to finish fifth, but not well enough to prevent a hefty hole being made in my pocket. Marshall was then training from the Eve Lodge Stable, the yard Lester Piggott had built about three years previously and from which he now trains with some success. Even then, if you happened to be wondering whether Lester was a millionaire yet or not, you just had to look at the set-up and estimate how much it must have cost to build a brand-new yard with eighty boxes in it and with automatic feeding devices.

As soon as I arrived on the course an hour before the first race I knew I'd done the right thing in not going to the Nassau Stakes at Goodwood. All the old faces were here. The first one I bumped into was the late Tommy Turner, who used to stand up on the rails for William Hill in the old days. Tommy was typical of the older generation of racing professionals. Under his soft brown hat there was a face as ripe as a windfall. I once saw him make a book at Worcester while at the same time, between races, he managed to consume an entire bottle of Courvoisier in the Members' Bar. I hasten to add it was an accurate book which showed the old firm a profit. Reminiscing about Worcester I remarked how odd it was that it was the only track in England that actually had a pub on the course itself. He said that sadly they'd pulled it down, but then he went on to tell me about the other convenience in Worcester. He said that there was a pub *inside* the cemetery grounds, which made it a very short journey if you weren't feeling up to scratch.

The first race was won by Etienne Gerard, a giant of a two-year-old, and it started a lot of arguments in the bar after. I'd always thought that Brigadier Gerard was a fluky horse and I was already convinced that it would be madness to pay vast sums for his progeny at that early stage of his career as a stallion. His sire, Queen's Hussar, was a goodish horse who threw a few goodish horses, but the Brigadier was the only really top class one. Well, I know he was more than top class. But he was a long way then from being proved as a great sire, and I'm sad to say that subsequently Brigadier Gerard's dismal career at stud has proved me to have been right on that rare occasion.

Bill Marshall bought yet another bottle of champagne when he heard that he had won the first race of the day at Thirsk with Minstrel Song, ridden by his son Richard. Then I went with him to watch him saddle up The Guvnor for the fourth race. It's always interesting to go with a trainer into the paddock and meet the jockey and listen to the riding instructions. Alan Bond had the mount, and there was a fair amount of optimism in the air that in receipt of two stone from Berkeley Square The Guvnor might bring it off. 'Keep him up with the others all the time, because he loves to be in the thick of things, and then see if you can make a run for it three furlongs out.'

At that moment, Rhodomontade's jockey walked by to mount his horse and Marshall said, 'Oh shit. He heard us.' This was followed by a lot of laughing and I felt as though I was in the middle of a schoolboy conspiracy. Sadly for all the connections, The Guvnor came third and Berkeley Square lived up to his name by demonstrating a fair amount of class.

Incidentally, the fortunes of Alan Bond in the ten years since that day at Newmarket illustrate as well as anything the ups and downs of racing. Bond had been champion apprentice in both 1974 and '75, in both years beating his nearest rival Richard Fox. When he was then invited by Henry Cecil to become the new stable jockey, the world seemed to lie at his feet. But his association with Cecil was short and disastrous and from then on it was all downhill. He rode fewer and fewer winners until at the beginning of 1987 it was announced he was leaving these shores to try and make a living somewhere else. And it wasn't because he lacked talent. Bad luck breeds bad luck and too much of that leads to you going out of fashion. There's nothing as unloved in racing as an unfashionable jockey, and when you're deeply unfashionable you may as well hang up your boots. Richard Fox, on the other hand, is currently a popular and successful lightweight.

I didn't have a bet in the next race but then at the very last moment, as they were going into the stalls for the sixth, I got hit over the head by a hunch and, running like Last Tycoon himself towards the bookies, I got a fiver on Bicoque. As they raced past us inside the final furlong it seemed like a mess of a blanket finish. Then they announced that Bicoque had won by a head. There was more agony to come in the form of a stewards' enquiry which went on for fifteen minutes and then they gave the all clear. Bicoque the winner at 33-1. But you know what really kills me about betting on the horses? You're never happy. I'm not, anyway. I sat there under the trees sipping the last dregs of the Bollinger, cursing myself for not having put a tenner on. It was pathetic, really, and got me to thinking that a psychiatrist I know probably hit the nail on the head when he described punting as 'collecting injustices'.

A couple of weeks later and I was bound for Newbury to back Oats in the Geoffrey Freer. A day at the races can be nearly made or broken by the race train. I had recently taken to this form of transport for two reasons. Firstly, I had sensibly decided to give up driving before I killed somebody. This, by the way, led to the necessity, when living in the wilds of Berkshire, of sending myself a postcard every day so that the postman had to drive out the three miles from the village to deliver it and I would get a ride back with him to the pub. Secondly, I had recently been driven to the races by the first English model to appear as a centrefold for *Playboy*. She was driving a brand new Aston Martin, and when I nervously complained about the speed we were going she said, 'Oh, I'm not in top yet . . .' She suddenly put it up to another gear that I hadn't imagined even existed and there we were doing a hundred and sixty down the M4.

When I first started going to the more distant courses by train some twenty years ago I looked forward to those journeys almost as much as I looked forward to the racing itself. Traditionally, the restaurant car to Salisbury, for example, would be taken over by bookmakers, their workmen – the tic-tac men, clerks, runners etc – the spivs and the touts. Out would come the cards for kaluki or gin rummy, and out would come the most fantastic yarns of villainy and chicanery that would keep me spellbound and laughing for most of the journey. On the return journeys, the generosity of the bookmakers would be, on occasions, stupendous.

At one time, the race trains to and from York during the August meeting were, I think, the only trains on British Rail to carry champagne. They didn't carry it for long. After Peterborough, the passengers carried it. Brighton races were almost worth going to for the journey alone and I once came back from Chepstow on a train that was something like a nightclub travelling at eighty mph. But it was not all fun. Some services were and are shameful. If you ever miss the first of the two trains that are the specials to Newbury, you might just as well forget it. I did just that on this occasion and found myself going down on a nasty, buffetless, corridorless pay-train of the sort British Rail lay on to give you an inkling of what it must have been like to have been a Jew in Germany a few years ago.

Anyway, once at Newbury the nasty taste of the journey

didn't in fact last very long. I kicked off with 10-1 winner Destino and there's no better way of starting a day. The winner of the first race always gives you the necessary confidence as well as the enemy's money to play around with. So when Oats got beaten a head and I lost only a tenth of my winnings it wasn't a knockout blow. I spoke to trainer Peter Walwyn after the race and he seemed pleased enough with the animal's performance. He said he'd go much better in the St Leger and with a month more to work on the horse, he was happy enough. Maybe, I began thinking, the money was only lent. Maybe. The winner Swell Fellow started at 16-1 and I felt rather bad about that one. Ten minutes before the off I had been talking to an ex-colleague, Alan Jamieson, who used to be on the *Sun*, when he turned to me and said, 'Shall I put my cash on Swell Fellow or buy a bottle of Bollinger?' 'Buy the Bollinger,' I told him, 'Swell Fellow's got no bloody chance.' Yes, well, people shouldn't listen to people, should they?

It was at that point that Roger Mortimer appeared at the bar and gave me a short but fascinating lecture on matters of stallions covering mares. His theory, an interesting one and one that might connect with humans possibly, is that a stallion needs to be something of a shit to be good at stud. He told me that the great racehorse The Tetrarch was very sweet-natured and found sex a most fearful bore. He only got a hundred and twenty foals, eighty of which won. When he covered a mare, apparently they had to keep dead quiet because if he heard someone sawing a piece of wood or drop a bucket, it put him right off. St Simon, on the other hand who was a bit of a bastard and who would eat a groom for breakfast, got five hundred and fifty foals. It reminds me of that great stallion Hyperion, who had an odd idiosyncracy for a horse. As a general rule, animals don't take in all that much that isn't immediate, but Hyperion, they say, in his old age, was fascinated by aeroplanes and if one flew overhead while he was covering a mare, he'd stop and follow it around with his head and eyes until it was out of sight.

But back to the races. The day continued well enough and in the fifth race Princess of Verona obliged at 3-1, but I was disappointed with the ladies on show that day. Now it's a fairly well-known fact that racing doesn't attract many grey people. Racing folk tend to be either the salt and mustard of the earth or they're utterly ghastly. But there used to be some wonderful-looking women at the racetrack. Where are they now? Discussing the serious shortage with a trainer at Newbury that day I was fascinated by the way – and it's simply a habit not an insult – he referred to them as though they were horses. I had observed this before though, come to think of it. I once asked Fred Winter what he thought of a certain trainer's mistress and he said, 'Oh, she's very moderate.' The trainer I spoke to that Saturday decribed one woman there as being 'of little account'. My day ended with buying a drink for one whom Mr Winter and his colleagues would describe as 'Promising, useful, scope'

bernard's guide to gambling types

The next time you go to the races resist the temptation to dive straight into the business of losing money for a few minutes and watch the various sorts of punters as they go about their business. There are eight types that I know of:

1. **The really big punter** is the one I most like to watch. He gambles vast sums and win or lose he looks incredibly bored with the whole proceedings. The braver bookies twitch nervously as he approaches, their brains rehearsing odds and fizzing with calculations in case he has a bet with them. He'll risk five grand in just the same voice as he'll order a cup of tea.

2. **Rich idiot**, I call him. A successful businessman who likes to gamble, but whose main motivation is to impress

Bernard's Gambling Types – No. 1

The Really Big Punter . . . gambles vast sums, and win or lose he looks incredibly bored with the whole proceedings.

whichever young girl he happens to be with. The girls with type two, incidentally, are either models, someone else's daughter, actresses, 'in showbusiness' or on holiday from Kenya. That's to say, amateur brasses. He'll always tell anyone who can be bothered to listen that he's very well up on the day.

3. **The non-punter**. He wanders round the paddock sucking thoughtfully on a cigar someone gave him pretending that he's trying to make up his mind which horse to bet on. In fact he's not going to bet on any of them. He imagines he might be mistaken for a wealthy and knowledgeable punter, or even an owner. On Monday morning he'll tell the receptionist at the second-hand car showroom where he works that he had a 'fair afternoon – not much, just a few hundred up'. She won't believe him, but won't bother to tell him so, either. He owes two weeks rent.

4. **The compulsive punter** is usually to be found in the Members' Bar, sweating, shouting, losing badly or winning as though it's his divine right. Very unsociable, impatient and intolerant of others, the indulges in boring post-mortems after the last race when everyone else is going home and his girlfriend has just left with type two.

5. **Women gamblers**. Your average one is probably between forty and fifty although she has the constantly-twitching but well-manicured hands of a woman of sixty. She chain smokes, uses too much perfume, wears too much jewellery and covers herself to an absurd extent with each-way bets. Don't try to talk to her. She'll think you're trying to pick her up. If you are, you'll have to earn every penny of it, and she knows all about gigolos. Her husband left her a million and she smiled all the way to the funeral, and now she's the sort of woman who has lunch alone at the Ritz. She's also a shrewd nut and probably wins in the long run.

6. **Young gamblers**. Japanese students, Persian remittance men, boys between public school and work, and boys between rich aunts and a carpet in Wandsworth

comprise this tiresome lot. There is admittedly the odd deb's delight or a redundant Rajah who finds the 2.30 at Kempton the nearest he can get to pig-sticking, but they're mostly amateur students. They haven't a quarter the amount of money they give the impression of having and they've seen someone win in the movies so they think they can. They're suckers for tips and think they can make a fortune backing favourites. They tend to pass out in the Gents, lose their girlfriends to types one, two, three and four and are usually going to see their probation officers when they say they're going to Fortnum's.

7. **I don't like to talk about this lot. I'm one of them**. They're simply out of their depths. They know they can't win, but they'll risk it 'just this once'. They bet beyond their means, go mad when they win and cry all the way home on the train when they lose. Their cup doth not runneth over and there's a nasty tendency towards bitterness which takes the form of swearing loudly in the Gents when it's empty. They also retreat there to have a private roll call of their rapidly dwindling wad from time to time. They gamble while under the influence of alcohol and/or the astrological columns and they're even mad enough to gamble to 'get out of trouble'. That's why they're always in it. Like most dogs they have their day. About once in a lifetime.

8. **Losers**. Losing is written right across the faces of some people, and it's hard to define. There's a slightly watery look about the eye and a tendency towards ash on the waistcoat or chipped nail varnish depending on the sex. There's a nervous twitch of the lips that promises to be a brave smile or the harbinger of tears – you can never tell which. There's the touching gesture of bravado in the form of a nonchalantly produced wallet that contains one last tenner. There's a seemingly wise and knowing nod of the head which is realy the burden of remorse. There's *Raceform* on the table at home with the last three weeks' installments missing. There's the old and faded trilby and the hired binoculars and the cigarettes plucked from packets of ten. At 6pm when they return to their dreadful little flat in Tooting even the cat knows they've lost. On

Bernard's Gambling Types No. 4

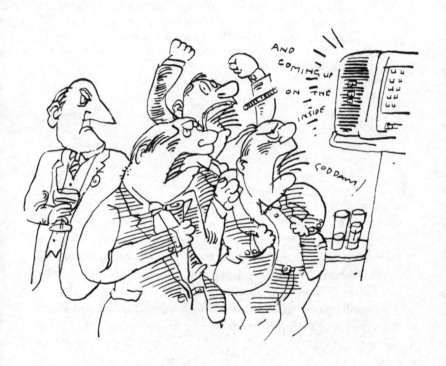

The Compulsive Punter is to be found in the Members' Bar, sweating, shouting, losing badly . . .

Monday at the office the clerk spots them looking at the day's runners at Southwell and Bangor. There's a Luncheon Voucher for lunch and then an afternoon of wishful thinking to be got through.

After that, it's gin and tonic time. Things don't seem to be so bad after all. Now's the time to flash the teeth in a brave smile and afford the big spender all the sympathetic laughter you can muster. You too can be a big spender. It's nearly payday anyway and you're due for a run of luck. Saturday could be the day. Just one brave bet at 20-1 could swing it. Just one selling-plater that stays the course. And may God have mercy on our souls.

2

A WEEK AFTER NEWBURY I HAD TO REVISE MY OPINIONS ON THE shortage of attractive women at the races when I went to Kempton Park. The feature race was the Playboy Nursery Handicap Stakes and, thanks to the sponsors, who are no longer in the bookmaking business, the course was liberally littered with bunnies. I examined one of these animals at moderately close quarters and came away full of admiration at the way they'd been turned out. Their costumes could have been designed by Brunel. The bra works on the cantilever system and is not so much a repository but more a launching pad. How apt then that their race should have been won by Showpiece, a bay colt by Daring Display out of Magic Thrust, and thanks be to the good goddess Venus that I had a fiver on it at 5-1. After the race there was a presentation in the unsaddling enclosure and then the photographers asked the late Sir Gordon Richards to pose for the odd snap with a bunny called Penny. This was an amazing sight. Sir Gordon, the best friend the punters ever had, was then in his seventies and had definitely stopped growing. His head came exactly level with Penny's cantilever constuction and try as the old maestro did to look her straight in the eye his twinkling orbs kept dropping to her Brunel-encased breasts.

Exhausted by this display of hypnotism, I sat down on a bench with a couple of jockeys outside the weighing room. It was much the same story there. I couldn't see a horse for the quantity of behinds. In front of me there was a wall of black-stockinged legs and white tails which played strange tricks with what little there was left of my concentration. Nevertheless, somehow I managed to follow Showpiece with Sousa who won the Geoffrey Hamlyn Handicap Stakes at 7-1. That was really thanks to his nicely unsecretive trainer, Michael Stoute, who dropped me a heavy hint earlier in the day that his horse would win. Now, ten years on, Stoute has twice been champion trainer, establishing a record for prize money won in one season in 1986, and is widely acknowledged as one of the great masters of his art.

By this time, I was on the crest of a tiny wave flecked with Louis Roederer spume and I was in half a mind to make a complete pig of myself by going on to the White City dog track, now sadly pulled down, after the last race at Kempton. But my old friend Chris Smith put me off. He's a tic-tac man and something of a character and when I asked him if he'd mark my card at the dogs later on he begged me to go straight home. 'Don't go to the dogs, don't go, son. You've got no bleedin' chance and I'm here to tell you that I owe every bookmaker on the bloody track.' I quote Mr Smith just to show you that bookmakers and their workmen get into just as much trouble as we mugs. Well, almost.

Not so long ago, there was a bookmaker with a chain of betting shops and a compulsion to play *chemin de fer* for very heavy stakes who was encouraged to go on playing up to the hilt so that the casino owners could step in and buy his betting shops for a rock-bottom price. Not many people are safe from gambling once they've tasted the delicious flavour of a big win

The Playboy Handicap

. . . the photographers asked the late Sir Gordon Richards to pose for the odd snap with a bunny called Penny. This was an amazing sight.

and bookmakers are no exception. Had I won a fraction more at Kempton Park I might have been tempted to go on to White City to lay a couple of short-priced favourites, but remembering the doleful look in Chris Smith's eyes I went straight home.

I was soon wishing I'd stayed at home on the Tuesday too instead of going to York for the first day of the big August meeting. Earlier in the season, on advance information from Chantilly, I had backed Empery ante-post to win the Derby at 20-1, so naturally I was looking forward to seeing my old friend again. The news that he wasn't after all going to run in the Benson and Hedges Gold Cup (now the Matchmaker International) wasn't the best start to the day that I could have wished for and then when Crow got beaten by Wollow I viewed the finish with mixed feelings. I had had a fair bet on Crow at 10-1, but on the other hand I was glad to see an English-trained horse win the race. I had mixed feelings about York in general terms too, as well as about the big race. It is without doubt one of the finest meetings in the calendar and the course is a cracker but it was so uncomfortable watching racing among so many people – about thirty thousand then and probably even more now – that I resolved to stick to the television at home in the future. It really isn't a sort of inverted snobbery that makes me prefer going to one of the 'gaffs' on a Wednesday or Thursday. The York people run the course very well and the atmosphere is always good, but all those people in the heat can make it a shattering day. Disaster was averted only by an invitation halfway through the afternoon from Bill Marshall to join him in the trainers' luncheon room.

On the next Saturday I attended the last evening meeting of the year at Windsor. They're odd things, evening meetings. The first race was at 5.30pm and the last one around 8pm. I'm not entirely sure I like them, although Windsor has its points. The executive at least seem to like racing, which is half the battle, but it feels slightly odd to start one's hooliganism at teatime. Royal Match won yet again and even though he was one of the best handicappers in training at the time he was such an incredible tribute to his trainer, the late Ryan Jarvis, that the horse just went on winning and winning. Ryan's son Willie has recently made a very bright start to his own training career. A former assistant to Henry Cecil, he now has a strike rate almost to rival his old guvnor and has already broken his duck at Royal Ascot with his smart colt Colmore Row.

That evening at Windsor, I had taken as my companion for the betting, one Fred Dipper, a pub acquaintance from Lancashire who bet in fifties and hundreds, in those days, and who didn't know the difference between those employed by United Dairies and those sired by Sea Bird II. Over the years I've bumped into a lot of characters like this one and they've all of them never failed to irritate me. Basically, they're men who gamble fairly heavily and with a modicum of success on a form of animated roulette that they don't understand. I'm beginning to twig the secret of their success. It's simply an utter contempt for money, regarding it simply as pieces of paper, and that in turn makes for supreme confidence. At Windsor that night, I tore a page from his book and found it rather nerve-racking. By the fifth race, I was so much down I was nearly drowning in self-pity and fiscal damage. Then I thought I'd put my betting boots on and wager like Fred. I had my last, but really my last, twenty-five pounds in the world on a one-paced horse called Sweet Reclaim and it just got up to win at 11-4 by half a length. I didn't want to go through that again. I decided to stick in the future to being pretentiously knowledgeable, and the heart and pocket would last much longer. Fred meanwhile has no doubt gone on backing winners out of sheer blind ignorance and nerve.

If you ever take anyone racing for the first time and, presumably, intend for them to like the business, then I must advise you not to try them out with Kempton Park. This is an extremely dodgy and usually rather boring racetrack. Of course, it has its compensations. There are bars, bookmakers, races that are won by winners and the grass is green, but my experience of it the Monday after the Windsor evening meeting, a Bank Holiday, made me more reluctant than ever to visit the place again.

The whole afternoon was so ghastly that not even the backing of Briar Patch, who won at 12-1, could entirely compensate for the hour of boredom and fuss that it took to reach the place and park the car, and the entrance money that it took to get into the Ring. Nerves were steadied and cooled by the sight of Briar Patch's trainer, the late Ryan Price. I'd been told he'd given a remarkable interview on television at York a few days previously in which he'd claimed to be a 'bloody genius'. Captain Price was without doubt one of, if not the most remarkable people in the business. I suppose what really used to upset the few people who were upset by him was the bald fact that he really was a genius or pretty close to whatever that may be.

He trained the first winner of the afternoon as well, which steamed in at 15-1. There was no stopping him in those days. And he seemed to be pretty sure that his Marquis de Sade would win the St Leger in a couple of weeks.

Half way through the afternoon I fell in with a big punting owner from Wales, Paddy Gallagher, who was unlucky enough to have his horse scratched from the big handicap of the day. Paddy had fancied it and I hate to think how much he would have put on it. Five years previously I had bumped into him at Sandown Park and he asked me to accompany him to the rails where he was going to collect from the bookmakers for a win he'd had the previous week with a hurdler at Cheltenham called Bumble Boy. I swear it took his man on the rails twenty minutes to count the stuff out. When I reminded him of the episode he rightly said, 'Don't forget the bad days.'

infantile megalomania

In my opinion the only point in betting is to earn money when you're skint. I bet because I'm greedy and want to get something for nothing. And a word of advice, ignore tips. The nearer to the horse's mouth, the worse they are.

It has been suggested that in a few hundred years' time gamblers will be forced by law to have psychiatric treatment. It's a very simple sickness, completely infantile for a start. It's also a chronic complaint that invariably lasts for life. The gambler, after all, is the one person who is completely unmoved by experience. In the beginning, it's a disease that's comparable to the megalomania that possesses all babies: when they want milk, they cry and they get it.

Where do I get all this from? The answer is Edmund Bergler, an American pshychoanalyst who wrote a book on the psychology of gambling. He says that the placing of a bet is an unconscious provocation of a situation wherein the gambler will be defeated. His hate-filled and seemingly self-defensive attacks on self-constructed enemies are made for the purpose of enjoying an unconscious masochistic pleasure. He could have fooled me. But I do realise that some gamblers want to lose. Time and time again I've noticed, and I don't need an analyst to point it out, that nearly all gambling reminiscences and post-mortems concern losses and not winnings. Invariably, when recollecting the past, gamblers will say: 'I'll never forget that day. I got beaten for a thousand quid by a neck and a short head.'

For some strange reason, punters have short memories when it comes to winnings. There are of course the odd exceptions that prove this rule. One of them is a man I know who is so clinically unique he should be stuffed and mounted in the Natural History Museum. In fact this is a very real possibility.

He devoted years to the formbook with little tangible success, but as luck would have it he did a ten-bob accumulator one day and won two thousand pounds. (This was many years ago.) He immediately gave up his job and flew his wife and mistress to the south of Spain, where they spent a happy month fighting over him and occasionally pouring bottles of cheap wine over his head. And of course that's where it all went. To his head, I mean.

He returned to England armed with an inordinate amount of conceit, arrogance, bitterness and fifteen shillings. He'd done it once, he said, and there was no good reason why he shouldn't do it again. Every day. The last I heard of him he was working as a messenger on a tit magazine. His classic case of paranoia and delusions of grandeur shuffled in with a persecution complex is typical of the sort of man who likes to think of himself as being a 'classical' gambler, according to Bergler.

This is simply the gambler who deceives himself that his gambling is an intellectual exercise, rather like a game of chess. Outwardly he gives the impression that he's desperately keen to win, but underneath he enjoys his daily stint of self-commiseration and he is, in fact, never happy until he has received his 'daily dose of injustice'. The classical gambler has a greater capacity for suffering than he has an ability to enjoy success.

I particularly like Bergler's summing up of the *real* gambler. He is marked by the following characteristics or clinical symptoms:-

1   Gambling is a typical, chronic and repetitive experience in his life.
2   Gambling absorbs all his other interests like a sponge.
3   He is pathologically optimistic about winning and never learns his lesson when he loses.
4   He cannot stop when he is winning.
5   No matter how great his initial caution, the true gambler eventually risks more than he can afford.
6   He seeks and enjoys an enigmatic thrill which cannot be logically explained since it is compounded of as much pain as pleasure.

I once had a friend, a compulsive gambler and habitual loser, who eventually cancelled his subscription to 'The Life' as it offered too much temptation. He further stated that he owed a lot of money and was being sued for the rates. 'There's one good thing about being skint though,' he told me. 'It keeps the mind lively and generally puts one on one's toes.'

Well, of course it does. I know it's an expensive way of keeping fit but, by God, it works. There's nothing like a bailiff on the doorstep or a brief in King's Bench to keep one up to the mark. I can recommend trouble for anyone who's complacent about life. Just think of the amount of winners that the Marchioness of Tavistock would suddenly have if she were overdrawn at Hambros, or the number of successes Charles St George would chalk up if the exhaust pipe on his Bentley fell off. It doesn't bear thinking about. If the roof fell in at Sunningdale, John Banks might even lay a loser.

It's not the sort of philosophy they teach at Trinity or Magdalen I know, but perhaps they should. If Lester's cigar had gone out and he wasn't offered a light, I'd hate to think what might have happened to Sir Gordon's record. No. It's obviously the thing to do. Go skint.

I remember having a perfectly miserable day at Fontwell Park one week, backing winner after winner until I met Jack Cohen. He bought me a drink, a cup of tea, a cigar and lent me the fare home. He then told me that I was a lousy good-for-nothing. Life suddenly had some sort of meaning again and it was a tremendous relief to back the last two losers. Oh yes. I shall always be grateful to him for that.

Once you are skint, all sorts of ways of trying to earn a bob or two come to mind. In the old days, people used to write begging letters, Bohemians in particular. I know one chap who used to average five a day, it didn't matter who to, just anyone from out of the telephone directory. Quite respectable people used to do it to vague acquaintances: 'I'm trying to write a book. Could you let me have five hundred quid? . . . ' But there are no longer the patrons like there used to be. There was one multi-millionaire a good few years ago who used to have a string of writers, some very famous, on his payroll, each receiving a fiver or a tenner a week. It used to make him feel good.

On the other hand Harry Diamond, the photographer, always walks along with his head held down at an odd angle. You think he's depressed or something when you first meet him. But he's not. He's watching the gutter,

Clinical Symptom of REAL Gambler No. 5

No matter how great his initial caution, the true gambler eventually risks more than he can afford.

hoping he might come across a fifty-pence piece. He once took a photograph of Frank Norman and me in Old Compton Street. I thought it was just some joky snapshot. The next day Harry came round and asked for ten pounds for the print. I gave him a fiver reluctantly, in fact very reluctantly. It now serves as a memento of the days when I thought that drinking whisky was some sort of a career.

Personally, I used to like to shoot craps. It's a marvellous game because you're participating yourself. It's not as if you're just being dealt the cards. The best game I ever had was in The Pair of Shoes in Hertford Street, quite a posh club years ago, which was run by Eric Steiner, a very nice man and a good punter, one of the few ever to beat Nick the Greek at cards. That was at poker in Las Vegas in the fifties. The game lasted three days and they just broke off occasionally to have a shower, a change of clothes and some eggs and bacon.

At the time of my big win in The Shoes I was on the bum, dishwashing. Eric knew this and for a few weeks before Christmas he'd been well aware of what was going on. The club served free drinks if you were punting. I used to go in and have a pound on red and a pound on black every night and so ate and drank for nothing, unless zero came up. One night I had had more than just the one. Playing craps, I had a fiver on seven and then passed out. Somone tapped me on the shoulder and woke me up to tell me seven had come up five consecutive times. That's got to be somewhere near a world record. I had an enormous pile of chips in front of me and luckily I had enough sense to cash them in and walk out. It was Christmas Eve and I was assured of enjoying myself after all. The only snag was that I left half my winnings in the bloody taxi.

There was another gambling club in Berkeley Square I used to frequent. Before his deportation, George Raft came up to me one night and told me Continuation would win the Royal Hunt Cup. I knew he knew bugger all about racing, but as he was a bit of a gangster I thought I'd put a fiver on it. It pissed in at 25-1 and the next week he left the country — in a hurry.

It's hard to understand why rich people still like to bet, but they do. Robert Sangster is a shrewd punter with a lot of nerve. I was having a drink with him at Newbury one September when Fred Binns walked past. Robert said, 'Oh, by the way Fred, while you're there, can I have £5000 to win Detroit in the Arc?' I asked him why he was putting five thousand pounds on his own filly to win a race that boasted prize money of a hundred and fifty thousand and would enhance her paddock value by a million or more. 'Just for interest's sake,' he replied. And I don't know whether it's true, but the Queen is reputed to have small bets on her horses. Just a tenner at a time. While Charles St George, a millionaire, does a yankee every Saturday.

3

WITH THE ST LEGER APPROACHING THAT DISMAL BANK HOLIDAY at Kempton soon faded from my memory. Despite trainers' tips for other horses I became more and more convinced that Crow, the French-trained and Yves Saint-Martin-ridden contender, would win. The St Leger, the last classic, comes in for a lot of knocking these days but it is still an important and significant event in the racing calendar. Several winners of the race in this century have become very important stallions and they include Bayardo – grandsire of Hyperion, Swynford, Hurry On, Solario and Fairway. More recently, the St Leger has been won by many good, and some great, horses and it seems strange that the race attracts so little enthusiasm, especially as it is often a very exciting contest to watch. The other French challenger that year was to be ridden by that very good French-based jockey, Bill Pyers.

I met Bill Pyers in Chantilly once and he was doing a stint behind the bar of the hotel I use there, The Hotel du Château. Pyers was acting barman because he said that Chantilly bored him, but on the whole I can recommend the place. The Hotel du Château is at the end of the town and it lies behind what the French call the stables and what looks a bit like Buckingham Palace. At the end of the racecourse there's the Château du Chantilly which looks like something out of a fairy story and there's a mist and dew on the course every morning, even during the hottest of summers. By the railway station, at the other end of the town, there's the café where all the jockeys, trainers and pressmen from Paris gather, drink and natter. Behind the scenes it's a very posh place. On one visit there I looked round the stables then run by Jean Michel de Choubersky and owned by Rothschild and I looked at the house at the end of the yard and remarked how lucky he was to have such a place to live in. He said it wasn't his house but the head lad's. Later, I had lunch at his château and when I left he gave me some advice about the return trip to London. 'When you go through Paris,' he said, 'why don't you drop into the Tour D'Argent? You can get a very nice snack there.' Well, thank you Jean. Anyway, it's nothing like any racing place in England, and if you're ever passing that way it's well worth a look.

So is Lambourn, and the Lurcher Show there, organised and run by Peter Tabor, an ex-assistant trainer of Fred Winter's, and held on the Sunday after my bad experiences at Kempton, was an event I shall remember for the rest of my life. They say that you should keep your horses in the worst company and yourself in the best. Well, as far as racing company goes I was certainly in the best on this occasion. There was a marvellous lunch *chez* Peter Walwyn and I took a look around the yard that houses the older horses before that. I don't know whether you've ever tried talking to horses but they don't take a lot of notice. That yard was full of friends with the exception of Après Demain, an old enemy who had cost me dear and one which I had backed for the last time on the day beore. I asked him about the twenty quid I had lost and got very little response.

After the dog show in a nearby field in which spectators overcome by fresh air and the beer tent kept falling asleep, there were a few drinks to be had by the side of Mr Walwyn's swimming pool. Walwyn himself appeared wearing trunks and, taking a running dive into the pool, he shouted, 'Thank you, English Prince.' It seems he shouts the same message every time he takes to the water. English Prince's Irish Derby victory paid for the pool. Après Demain, I thought bitterly, hadn't paid for the tonic water that was consumed around the edge of it, the bastard. Anyway, sitting there with Joe Mercer and Jimmy Lindley and Edward Underdown was a very pleasant way of passing the evening, especially as Lindley and Mercer both backed up my opinion that Crow would win the St Leger. Even Fulke Walwyn spoke to me, and he hadn't done that for five years, since I'd remarked that his famous chaser The Dikler looked like a cart horse and he had got very upset.

This event had taken place in Lambourn one morning when I happened upon a rustic scene full of old-world charm and reminiscent of a Constable water-colour. Two men stood holding two horses by the verge in the lane opposite the Malt Shovel. The horses were eating grass contentedly and I noticed that one of them, on closer inspection, was one of the most magnificent cart horses I'd ever seen. They munched away, the birds sang in the trees, and I exchanged 'good mornings' with the stable men. Then I said: 'That's a nice looking horse you've got there,' pointing to the monster one, and added, 'I should think he could plough a field by himself in ten minutes.' At this, the horse looked round at me, made a nasty noise and then tried to kick me into the Malt Shovel before gargling time. I was extremely frightened, broke out into an immediate sweat and cowered in the doorway of the pub. I'm frightened of horses, it should be known, but this one was terrifying. The man soothed him, turned to me and said, 'This is The Dikler.' Well, Fulke Walwyn is just about the greatest trainer of jumpers there's ever been and I need hardly remind myself or you that about two years after that incident

The Dikler went on to win chasing's Blue Riband, the Cheltenham Gold Cup. But I still think he was a horrible-looking animal.

The Malt Shovel is a very pleasant little pub opposite Fulke Walwyn's yard. What's nicer about it than a London pub is standing in the window and watching his and Fred Winter's strings walking back after working on the Downs. What you mustn't do if you go there is to take notice of everthing you hear. You can be given fifty tips in the time it takes to drink a pint of beer with the stable lads. You can then move on to the Red Lion and get another fifty tips to beat the fifty you just got. But still, it's a pleasant way to pass a morning.

I'm happy to say that Crow subsequently won the St Leger, but the race had complications. I had lunch with a man shortly afterwards who is well known in racing circles, has sponsored an important race or two and has friends in well-manured places. Another French horse in the St Leger, Campero, had run like a pig, but his connections had vehemently denied that the horse had been doped. My informant told me otherwise.

Before the race, two of the French challengers, Campero and Secret Man, had run against each other and finished within one and a half lengths of each other on two occasions. That year the St Leger was run on 11 September and, ten days before that, Campero stood at 8-1 in most of the ante-post lists and Secret Man at 9-1. On the day of the race, Campero opened at 7-1 and started at 9-1. Secret Man, on the other hand, opened at 8-1 and started at 15-2. In the event Crow won easily enough from Secret Man, but Campero was beaten by approximately thirty lengths. *Raceform* said, 'Campero looked well, prominent till the eighth furlong, beaten in straight.' There are no more reliable publications in racing than *Raceform*, both the formbook and the red *Notebook*.

My informant went on to tell me that he was in the presence of Campero's connections and, although he admits that they're lousy losers on the other side of the Channel, he says that they were shocked, flabbergasted, amazed, choked and puzzled. The horse had been aimed at the St Leger for ages. They expected it to run really well. At least, Maurice Zilber, the horse's trainer, did.

Now it so happens, and this is where there might be a little crunch, that days after, when Zilber was talking to the owner, the latter owned up to having had thirty thousand pounds to win on Campero. This is quite surprising and not a very small bet for a businessman to have on the first horse he'd ever owned. When you consider that the same owner,.to the best of Zilber's knowledge, had never been on a racecourse before, then you realise that it was an enormous bet even by old-fashioned standards.

When I was told this, I immediately asked my informant, 'How could he get such a bet on?' since bookmakers, generally speaking, lost their nerve in the 'thirties'. Well, he said, he'd checked on that and all the big boys had admitted that it had been a particularly strong market for the St Leger. Lots of people had shovelled it on that year.

Now it was odd that all the doped horses that season – as far as one could tell, that is – had been doped to win and not to lose. How then did anyone get at Campero to stop it? It must have been got at over here in England. Remembering that Jockey Club security had had well-publicised lapses, it was fairly safe to assume that someone got at the beast at Doncaster itself. When? When the horse was at exercise. How? Easily. By putting something in the manger. How? Easy again. It was a fact then, even if it might be a little more difficult now, that any man carrying a bucket in one hand and preferably wearing a cloth cap could get into anywhere where they kept valuable racehorses in this country.

If you don't believe that, I can tell you that I had recently spent an undisturbed half-hour in a yard that housed what then must have been five million pounds worth of horseflesh. One man looked at me and said, 'Mornin' guvnor,' and another just grinned at me and went on his way. I know, for a fact, that you can't do that on courses like Longchamp. I also know, for a fact, that ten years ago you could wander fairly freely around stable courses in this country. So anyway, *who* had Campero stopped?

Obviously that's what was intriguing, and still is, because once you've cleared the owner and trainer the field is wide open. I'll tell you another thing about bookmakers and, hoping you've worked out that thirty thousand pounds at 8-1 is a liability of two hundred and forty thousand pounds, a very good friend of mine had recently reported the not unusual sight of one of the biggest bookmakers in the country having lunch with one of the best jockeys in the country in one of the best restaurants in the country. I wouldn't be at all surprised if he still doesn't retain a couple to pull the odd favourite, but that's another matter . . . And remember, if you back losers and whether they've been doped or not, then there are sound-proof booths for moaners. Meanwhile, I was forming the opinion that if there was a guard dog with teeth in Newmarket and a watchman who was not permanently sloshed at Chantilly, then Welsh Flame might win the forthcoming Cambridgeshire, and Ivanjica the Prix de L'Arc de Triomphe.

pulling the fast one

It's not only trainers and jockeys who resort to sharp practices, gamblers cheat too. I suppose the most common scam used to be betting after time. In America, some time ago, they went to an enormous amount of trouble to get the man who relayed the racecourse commentaries to the bookmakers' offices to delay his commentaries for just one minute. They cleaned up packets before they were tumbled. There are endless dodges used by betting shop employees to mistime bets and you might wonder why they bother since they always get caught. It's the really petty stuff that intrigues me, though. A friend who is an ex-runner for a bookie told me a fairly sordid story when I last met him. He said he was standing in a pub one day where he used to take bets when a woman said to him that he'd dropped something and pointed to a bit of paper on the floor. Without much thinking he thanked her, picked it up and put it in his pocket. Of course, it was a slip for a race that had just been run. He found out later that her husband got the results on the phone, she'd then write out a winning bet and drop it on the floor by the nearest bookmaker.

The same man also told me about the strange graffiti on the wall of the Gents in a south London pub. He was idly gazing at it one day during an inter-race slash when he noticed that nearly all the words written had more than four letters. They were in fact the names Gentle Art, King's Petition and Prince Pan, which is exactly how they finished in the 1963 running of the Woodcote Stakes. Someone had been very fly in getting the results on the dot, tearing down to the Gents to write them up on the wall where someone else would come in and see them and write out a quick bet after time. Oddly enough it never occurs to this friend of mine to admit that he was a bit of a mug. I'm less surprised than he is that he is no longer in the bookmaking business. Incidentally, he's a very strange bird indeed. He now manages an old people's home, but he's always got wads of readies on him when he comes up to the West End. I suspect that quite a few wills are written in his favour by people who discover too late that he's standing on the oxygen tube. But that's another matter.

The coup I liked the best that never came off was the Francasal affair. If you don't remember it, they put in a ringer at Bath one day, cut the telephone wires to London so that the money couldn't get back and spoil the price and then they plunged on the horse which was returned, I think, at 100-8. The only other method I know of backing winners is to study form and take no notice of anyone. I've been doing that for years and the larder is still empty.

4

BEFORE TRYING OUT MY HUNCHES FOR THE CAMBRIDGESHIRE and the Arc de Triomphe, it was time to cross to Ireland for the Irish St Leger. There are things and people that can only happen over there and the place was still the friendly madhouse it has always been. At Waterford, where I first stopped for a couple of nights, I visited a golf club and saw a painted notice at the entrance of the place that would make an English golfer turn pale with horror. The notice said, 'Members are forbidden to train geyhounds on the links.'

It was wonderfully typical of the country. Inquiring about the notice I learned that the procedure was one of getting the dog you really wanted to work out to run with two others. What they do is to get someone to stand on the green and wave a handkerchief at the men holding three dogs on the tee. The men on the tee let one go and then another and when the first one's gone fifty yards they let the important dog go another fifty yards later. Apparently the third dog tries like a lunatic to catch up the other two and the gallop, as it were, brings him on a ton. When I asked the man who took me up to the place whether the other members got annoyed at this sort of activity he told me that, no they didn't, they just leant on their clubs and made rapid bets as to whether the third dog would catch the other two.

What was so Irish was that the man who introduced me to the place was a local and highly respected doctor who had been temporarily barred from my hotel for three months for breaking a chandelier in the restaurant. You could look for years, and sadly without success, in England to find a doctor like that. The good doctor also happened to own a load of property and a bar that I reckon was one hundred yards long. He told me that he thought it would be a nice idea to have his own place to drink in, had bought it for thirty-five thousand pounds, spent the same amount on it and was now going in for breeding cattle. Someone else said they thought he'd be a millionaire within five years, and then they introduced me to the local big deal dentist.

By the time I met him there'd been three races at Newbury, he was a hundred and fifty quid down and he couldn't stand up. He mumbled something about wanting a 'getting out' bet, so I told him what I thought might win the next. It lost. He lost another fifty quid and staggered off into the early afternoon. Just after that bit of disaster someone else came into the bar and told me that the waiter in the hotel had been easvesdropping on our conversation over breakfast and, thinking that three English racing journalists might know what they were talking about, had followed our tips. He went down by no less than three hundred pounds.

I couldn't believe it at first. I mean, can you imagine an English waiter with enough nerve to bang on three hundred pounds hearsay? Anyway, the two days in Waterford ended in disaster. We drove up to the Curragh on Saturday morning with empty pockets and sore heads. Both were soon revived. At the Curragh I was treated like visiting royalty in the way that the Irish always treat nonentities. I was taken to the oak-lined, champagne-filled, private rooms occupied by the men that ran the course. Compared to England it was an unbelievable scene. They wouldn't even let the Stewards of the course in the place it was so posh and yet there I was drinking what they called shampoo with the director of the course, Joe McGrath, and his brother the director of the Irish Hospital Sweeps, Paddy McGrath, who was reputed to have one hundred and fifty million in his current account. He turned to me half way through the afternoon and said, 'I can't understand why they call us the McGrafia.' Then he told me he couldn't sell or buy shares without the knowledge of it sending firms broke or ridiculously up-market.

For the two hours before the St Leger itself we all scanned the form to try to find something that would beat the odds-on favourite Meneval. I opted for Navarre. Meneval won easily, smoothly and by eight lengths. Piggott won three races altogether during the afternoon and I wasn't on a single one of them. Lesson. Don't be greedy. Short-priced winners are better than any kind of loser and it's as well to remember that not only do you win a little, but you actually get your wretched stake back. That night in Dublin the doctor came to the rescue with a financial injection. I said that I was a bit sick of racing and just wanted to go out and have a drink in those haunts where I'd drunk with the likes of Behan years before.

'A drink,' he said. 'Well, you'll be needing twenty pounds.'

'No,' I said, 'a drink means about five pounds.' (This was all of ten years ago, remember.)

'You might run into trouble,' he said and pressed the twenty quid into my hand.

'And when will you be wanting it back?' I asked, slipping into Irish.

'Next year at Royal Ascot,' he said.

Of all people who take themselves too seriously, the English racing classes ought to plead guilty and I mean more guilty than even those in the entertainment business. Offer some criticism to a jockey, poke some fun at a trainer and the heavens open up. I was once told I was responsbile for one trainer's heart attack. I had simply remarked, somewhat facetiously, that he covered the distance of ground between his yard and his local pub at a speed reminiscent of The Tetrarch. (He should have been so well bred!) The man exploded and apparently made some remark to the effect that trainers of racehorses were due respect because they trained racehorses. Well, well. What a funny lot some of them are. The trouble is that most of the genuinely funny ones are across the sea in Ireland.

Take Mick O'Toole. I once stayed the weekend with him at the Curragh. They're two days I shall never forget, though I can't remember them. He showed me round his yard on the morning I arrived. I used to pretend to be knowledgeable about horses on appearance, but I'm not. That's something you have to be brought up to. But on this occasion I was showing off, pretending I knew. Mick pulled a horse out of a box and said, 'There's a nice little fella here we've got.'

'He looks very good,' I replied. 'He looks as though he should stay three miles.'

Mick's retort was to the point. 'Jesus, Jeffrey, you're a fool. He couldn't stay bloody two miles in a fucking horsebox.'

Then we went to the pub. His wife prevailed on us to be back for lunch: 'There's a lovely joint in the oven . . . ' The pub was owned by Pat Eddery's father, Jimmy, and we arrived at opening time. Mick cautioned me: 'The old woman, she really means it. I daren't mess up the lunch. We can only have the one.' We were still there seven hours later.

The next day – it must have been about ten minutes away – he took me to the dogs in Dublin at Selhurst Park. Now since O'Toole was at one time in his early days a dog trainer I was more than eager that he should mark my card. He was quick to reassure me: 'You've got nothing to worry about, Jeffrey, just follow me.' My resources were limited. I was there on feeble expenses from some magazine. There were eight dog races that night and I backed everything Mick told me to. Together, we backed eight consecutive losers.

He was tremendously amused by our going skint, but I found it very hard to raise a smile since I have a genuine loathing for running out of money when I'm abroad. Actually, I'm not that fond of running out of money at Harringay, Ascot or in my betting shop, but giving handouts to bookies in Ireland or the Paris-Mutuel in France is ghastly. Anyway, O'Toole whistled all the way back to the Shelbourne hotel with me whining beside him: 'I just don't know what to do, Mick. You've screwed me up completely. I haven't got a pot to piss in.' I've never seen a man raise a float so quickly as he did. Within three minutes his pockets were running over and he 'saw me alright'. I tried to pay him back a day or so later but he refused: 'Keep it, Jeffrey. You don't owe me anything. You're a guest in my country.' He has a lot of friends does Mr O'Toole, he puts his money where his mouth is when he has a bet and I've never known the man complain when his horses do get stuffed.

I'd very much like to take a few of the humourless and pompus English trainers over to the Curragh and around his yard to show them that you don't have to imitate Colonel Blimp to train horses. Con Collins who trains over there is another case, and he has extraordinary ideas of what hospitality consists of. When I called in at his establishment I was shown into a sitting room and then a maid came in carrrying a tray on which were poised a glass, a bottle of Scotch whisky, a bottle of Irish, a bottle of gin, a bottle of brandy and a bottle of vodka. 'Mr Collins will be with you in five minutes and he says you're to ring the bell if you need any more to drink', she said.

I was still musing about the different types you meet in racing when I attended the Newmarket sales soon after the Irish St Leger. I only saw one record broken and that had nothing to do with horses. The record in question was a drink one. I saw one trainer from the West Country move into the bar at 10am, buy himself a large whisky and sit rooted to the spot for five hours without budging except to replenish his glass. This beat, by two hours, a record I'd seen set by an Irish trainer six years previously at Ballsbridge. Now I'm not sitting in judgement on the man, particularly since it took me five hours of my own time to observe, console and accompany him. The method is surprisingly successful, though on the face of it you'd think it would be tremendously difficult to buy, let alone bid for, a horse if you don't see one and aren't in the ring.

For all his five-hour sessions in the bar, my boozy friend is the heart and soul of racing. He once won one of the biggest handicaps in the calendar, only had fifty quid on the horse and celebrated the victory for four weeks. He treats his staff well, tells his owners they're fools if they are and by so doing loses their custom, and he's ridden over the sticks himself and broken more bones than banks. He never moans when he has a bad run and he doesn't gloat when he beats his colleagues and rivals. He doesn't suffer rich fools gladly and so he's unfashionable. When he does train a winner, the butcher, baker and garage-keeper appear at his backdoor within four hours. He lends impecunious stable boys money, gives handouts to anyone in the business who needs them if he can and he cries all the way to the bank. He's in his fifties now and it's unlikely he'll ever strike it rich, but he can show the young trainers a thing or two. Thank God for him, and for making the sales, the courses and the bars worth visiting.

the good, the bad and the ugly

Trainers, by and large, move in mysterious ways. Originally they were known as 'training grooms'. The title was appropriate. They fed and cantered the horses and took their orders from owners who knew as much about the business as they did. It was the Hon George Lambton who first made racehorse training a posh occupation round about the turn of the century. It was he, by the way, who made my favourite snob remark of all time. As an undergraduate at Cambridge he rode regularly to Newmarket to ride work, and one day on the Heath a gentleman work-watcher asked him what college he went to. 'I don't know,' replied Lambton, 'Trinity I suppose.'

Since then the training of horses has gathered about it an utterly disproportionate glamour – equalled only by the ridiculous reverence heaped on fashion photographers who are known to sleep with their models. I fancy you detect a note of sour grapes in my tone; if there is one, then it is because I'm fairly convinced that with the help of a good Irish head lad I too could train the likes of a Nijinsky, a Sea Bird II or a Shergar. In fact, I'm pretty sure that a horse of the stamp of Nijinsky could be galloped up the side of a slag heap every morning and still win the Derby.

Perhaps it's not quite as simple as that, and yes, of course, there are trainers who are tremendously skilful. Richard Hannon is one. He has won the Two Thousand Guineas twice, both times with comparatively cheap horses – Mon Fils and Don't Forget Me. Cheap horses are a feature of his Marlborough yard. He often takes on the bigger, classier yards and beats them. Such has been his success that he is now capable of training more winners then any but the ten or so biggest stables in the country.

Quite apart from his brilliance as a trainer he is also an unusually inventive gambler. About ten years ago his wife had triplets, two boys and a girl. One night after his wife and children had gone to bed, Richard was downstairs enjoying a drink with a merry band of lunatic, punting-mad Irishmen when he had a brilliant idea. He crept upstairs, got hold of the triplets, brought them down to the sitting room and arranged them on the sofa. 'Now,' he announced, 'we're going to play Find the Lady.' So there were the triplets gurgling happily on the sofa while all around them Richard's Irish friends were bunging on ten-pound notes, twenties, fifties, until finally a fortune had piled up on each of the babies. Then Richard would remove their nappies with a flourish and pay the punters who had found the lady. Then the game would start again: 'All out of the room,' Richard would bellow, 'while I shuffle them.' This marvellous source of income naturally came to an end when the babies grew old enough for their sexes to become too obvious, but before then fortunes were gambled on this real-life version of the three-card trick.

Richard got very merry when Mon Fils won the Guineas at fifty to one. 'Fuck you all,' he told the press. 'I'll never have to work again.' Of course he was back at the yard on Monday morning as usual.

I used to go to the sales with Dave Hanley, Eddie Reavey, Richard Hannon and my friend from Lambourn Doug Marks. On one occasion one of their number, I won't say who, never actually clapped eyes on a horse. He was in the bar all day every day for three days. But he consulted the catalogue from time to time and, on the strength of the breeding alone, sent someone out to bid for him. He ended up with a couple of decent animals and, as I've already said, it is a system I can recommend, especially to those trainers whose yards are stuffed with hand-picked million-dollar purchases that look good but won't do a tap.

Hanging round the sales is where you meet racing characters more than on the track, and you really do meet some idiots. How they get to be entrusted with millions of pounds worth of horseflesh is one of racing's enduring mysteries. Typical of this sort is the young, arrogant trainer who treats the stable lads the way he treated fags at school. There's even a PR man in the business who's so shabby that when he was an assistant trainer he actually did beat his stable staff. Anyway, this young idiot trainer appears at the sales in the morning in jodhpurs, roll-neck jersey and Barbour and immediately drops house points for boasting about his hangover. He then spends most of the morning trying to ingratiate himself with anyone with a title and more than a hundred thousand in his account. A disgusting sight.

In the afternoon he appears on the stands in a curly-brimmed soft hat and sounds off at full volume in an accent borrowed from St James's Street until about nine in the evening, at which time the wheels fall off his act and he roars off with his chums to some unspeakable olde worlde pub masquerading as a restaurant. Here they revert to prefect days at school, chuck bread rolls at people and scream at their lady friends, all of whom are called Arabella or Emma.

I know one trainer of this type who managed to book Lester Piggott to ride one of his horses. He had a hefty punt on it, but they were beaten a neck. This twit said to Lester afterwards: 'That's it, Lester. You'll never ride for me again.' Dry as you like Lester replied: 'Oh well, I'd better hang up my boots then, hadn't I?'

A band of trade union officials once bought a horse and sent it to this same idiot. One day they organised a coach trip to the yard to see the animal. There were two coach loads of proud, expectant owners, armed with sandwiches and Thermos flasks, all set for a visit to the stables to see their noble beast followed by an excellent day at the races, all for two quid a head. When they arrived at the training establishment, nothing stirred. Not a cock was crowing, not a stable lad in sight. Baffled, perplexed, they piled out of the coaches and wandered up to the house. They looked through a downstairs window. All they could see was their chosen trainer, in his dinner jacket, lying on a sofa and snoring, two empty champagne bottles on the table beside him. His career as a trainer was short-lived.

I don't want to give the impression that every trainer is a sozzled prat who looks as if someone's just waved a British Rail Race Day 'Special' pork pie under his nose. Take Bill Marshall, for instance, one of the most likeable characters of the Turf. He flew his own Spitfire from South Africa to England in 1940 and said to the RAF: 'Here's a plane and here's a pilot. Help yourself.' He shot down plenty of German planes and was awarded the DFC. Eventually he was shot down himself and was incarcerated in a prisoner-of-war camp. Needless to say he escaped, walked from Bavaria to the north coast of France, nicked a boat and made it back to England. He couldn't speak a word of German and so anyone who asked awkward questions on the way was making a big mistake. Bill used to train at Edenbridge, from where he sent out Raffingora to break the course record at Epsom over five furlongs (hand timing) and thus become the fastest horse in the world. He's only a tiny skinny fellow, but not one to provoke. After he moved to Newmarket he had a row with a colossus of a lorry driver who was trying to dump some supplies Bill hadn't ordered. When things got really heated, Bill simply laid him out with a punch that wouldn't have disgraced Sugar Ray Robinson.

He was one of the very few trainers who actually rode work rather than watching from the back of a hack. Some days he used to ride out three lots, not bad for a man in his fifites. Some of the old brigade of Newmarket trainers thought he was a bit of a nut, but Bill used to say it kept him fit and cleared the liver of any left-over champagne. When he retired he went to Barbados to sit in the sun and drink rum. But he soon got bored of that and now, aged about seventy, he is champion trainer over there. When not working he can be found sitting on a boat with a fishing rod in one hand and a rum punch in the other muttering to himself, 'This is the life.'

I can never understand how some of the biggest trainers who have up to two hundred horses in their yards keep track of them all, but you can't argue with success – look at Henry Cecil, he trains enough horses to fill the card at Newmarket for an entire season. And yet the man has a compulsive habit of collecting white shoes and is tee-total – which, I am reluctant to say, gives the lie to the idea that water is the refuge of half-wits. Barry Hills commands a similarly huge operation at Robert Sangster's complex at Manton. Hills made his money on a horse called Frankincense, which he backed down from 66-1 to 100-8 to win the Lincoln, enabling him to rise overnight from travelling head lad to trainer. That's the sort of story that makes people like me broke.

I suppose you have to love horses to be any good with them, and I don't. The girl who did the late Ryan Price's national winner Kilmore was so deeply attached to the animal that she wanted to take it on holiday with her. 'Where the hell are you going to go?' the Captain asked. 'Well, Guvnor, I'm going to a hotel in Bournemouth and I though he could stay on the lawn outside.' He was a great character, Ryan Price. He once employed a stable girl who was rather well-endowed. When he saw her having difficulty mounting a horse he would shout: 'Just throw your tits over and the rest will follow.'

But it doesn't do to get too obsessed with racing at the expense of everything else, though I don't see why you should take that sort of advice from me. One day I was being driven back from the races by an old pisspot of a trainer along with his wife Maisy and one of the gutsiest jockeys ever, whom I'd better call K, a real tough nut. He used to kick dead-beat horses into enormous fences in an absurdly fearless manner, but that day he'd ridden one of this trainer's horses without success. Anyway, this trainer and I were in the front of the car, with Maisy and K in the back. Maisy had her head concealed under an old tartan blanket and it was quite clear to me what was going on. The poor old trainer was rambling away about horses as usual: 'You know, K, I think perhaps we ought to try that horse over a different trip next time . . . Give him two and a half miles in the soft and he could be anything, especially if we let him make his own running . . . ' It was lucky he was talking to K not Maisy. Her mouth was full, and it wasn't a lollipop she was sucking.

5

THE FLAT SEASON EVENTUALLY CAME TO AN END, PRODUCING ITS usual bag of mixed results. In the Cambridgeshire, Welsh Flame ran as though he was carrying two tons through a bog. I had a nice win at the Arc de Triomphe, but then dropped the lot on the Dewhurst. I'll save the details of my disastrous Champion Stakes day, experienced from the not so safe distance of Soho, for later. It was now time to turn the attention to the jumps. I was soon wishing that it wasn't.

The poshest racecourse in England, Ascot, has an extraordinary grandstand. As far as I'm concerned it's a multi-million-pound concrete shambles. On Black and White day, at the end of November, I met at least six people who'd got lost in it. The escalators make it seem like something between an air terminal and a modern hospital. Come to that, I suppose it's a bit like a large store with no goods. Anyway, that's not my main beef. Neither is the fact that there are more bars in the grandstand than there are pubs in Brighton.

What I can't stand about the place is that it's so bloody hard to win money there. The horse cracked up by so many as being the star of Fred Winter's stable was not only returned at an unbackably short price, it then got well and truly outstayed by a rival. By the time Napoleon Brandy had been beaten in the second race I was making full use of the bar facilities in that dreadful stand. It was then that one of Toby Balding's owners came to my rescue. His name was Harry Beccle and he saved the day for me. Harry is an Eastender who'd already done pretty well for himself, well enough anyway to send his son to a posh prep school. When he went to watch him run in the hundred yards, surrounded by po-faced parents, he suddenly heard to his horror his own voice screaming out, 'Come on my son!' A dead give-away if ever there was one. He even managed to make me laugh when the wrong horse won the big race. By this time I was thinking of taking a part-time job, but I still didn't realise that I was about to lose more than I'd ever lost in one day's racing.

Meanwhile, Harry went on laughing at his own jokes and when someone picked him up on it he said with incredible logic, 'I laugh at my own jokes because it's the first time I've heard them.' By now I was falling for that silly old thing of picking prices and not horses, and by backing to get out of trouble I was getting deeper into it. I managed to forget my troubles for a few minutes when a lot of us watched the Night Nurse v Bird's Nest race on television. I looked at Bob Turnell's face as much as I looked at the television set: watching a trainer's face when he's got something in a big race is one of my favourite occupations. I stood next to Bernard van Cutsem a few years ago when his two-hundred-and-ten-thousand-pound charge Crowned Prince got stuffed at Newmarket. It was unnecessary to look at the race. I could read it in his face. As the face got longer, I knew that Crowned Prince was finding nothing.

On this occasion when Bird's Nest came to the second flight from home, Mr Turnell's entourage started bobbing up and down. By the time he cleared the last they were jumping up and down, almost hitting the ceiling. Bob Turnell was one of the greatest National Hunt trainers in post-war years. I am one of the greatest losers.

I'd arrived at Ascot determined to back one particular horse. Harry put me off it, and it was all his fault. Another runner couldn't be beaten, he said, and I went along with him especially since it was a better price. What folly, what insanity. I was now breaking into the weekend money, having done the housekeeping money after losing the gas and light money. With one race to go Harry was still laughing – I think his pockets might have been deeper than mine – and I was near tears. Fred Winter's representative was a certainty for the last race. Everyone knew it. So it was the second horse of the day to start at an unbackable price. Of course, what I should have done was to shovel everything on, float a quick loan and bang that on too. But off I went looking for outsiders again. It's a funny thing that it never occurs to one, when one's having a nervous breakdown that is, that outsiders are outsiders because they're not very good. So I backed almost everything in the wretched race that was more than 6-1.

I couldn't even bring myself to watch it. I stood on a balcony and took the occasional peep round the corner while hoping that the racecourse commentator had got his colours confused. But, damn it, the last peep I took revealed the unmistakable colours of the favourite zooming across the finishing line like Ribot. By now it was getting dark. The champagne was running out and a sausage roll left over from some other meeting was playing havoc with my guts. The girl I was with was looking at me with more disbelief than pity. I made the usual futile remarks about Monday being another day and Harry quite rightly pointed out that so was Tuesday.

Switching to large ports to fend off the evening air and general *angst*, we stayed in the bar until the course was almost deserted. I sat there uttering the usual clichés about racing teaching one to lose. Suddenly, for the life of me, I couldn't see what was so good about learning to lose.

It was a different woman who accompanied me to Sandown Park the next week, and she'd never been racing before. It's always fascinating in a ghastly sort of way to take someone to the races for the first time because they inevitably ask such daft questions. At one point this particular lady asked me why did the horses have tissue paper stuck to the inside of their hind quarters. I couldn't think what the hell she was talking about, gingerly approached the rear end of a horse in the

Black and White Day, Ascot

BEFORE   AFTER

Another runner couldn't be beaten, he said, and I went along with him especially since it was a better price. What folly, what insanity.

unsaddling enclosure and realised she was referring to the white foam that horses sweat.

She did make the interesting observation that racing people look conspiratorial, tend to talk out of the side of their mouths and invariably look as though they're up to no good. I've got so used to them that I don't notice, but she was right. A jockey we were with that day talked to us as though he was operating a ventriloquist's dummy and it was while sitting with him that I had the month's most embarassing moment. An owner new to racing joined us at our table in the bar. Thinking himself a bit of a lad, he suddenly leant forward and said to this jockey, 'I suppose you've pulled a few in your time?' This is roughly like asking a police officer, 'Taken any good bribes this week?' The amount of people in racing who don't engage brain before operating mouth sometimes seems to grow daily.

For the first three races my companion attempted to pick the winners by what she called cosmic means. When that failed, she turned to astrology. I pointed out to her that the sun signs method might be slightly unbalanced since horses are born in the first half of the year leaving everything from Leo to Sagittarius pretty blank. When I told her, just to make conversation mind you, that Park Top and I shared a birthday on 27 May she became even more convinced that it was all in the stars. I'm glad to say that she then went completely skint.

Two questions that newcomers to racing are continually asking is 'What's going to win?' and 'What won?' You might think that when something wins by ten lengths or so that it would be unnecessary to ask, but they always do. The other thing they always tell you is what a wonderful life you lead if you write about racing. There's an assumption that you never back losers and that the champagne in the Members' Bar is free.

'Why don't you ask that trainer what's going to win?' is another phrase that keeps popping up. I never ask trainers for tips and I've always been convinced that it's bad form. Why the hell should any trainer tell the world when he thinks he might have a touch? I'd keep very quiet about it if I trained and thought I had something that might win the next at 10-1. In fact, trainers in this country are tremendously co-operative with the press. In France they show journalists round the back to the tradesmens' entrance.

After the last race we dillied and we dallied in the bar with a few of the spivs and the touts and the lady then told me what wonderful warm human beings they were. She obviously thought it was just like *Guys and Dolls*. I pointed out to her on the way home that they were desperate men who'd been up to more tricks and dodges than she'd dreamt of, but she wasn't having any of it. I then realised that she'd unknowingly become hooked on racing and in only one afternoon. I suppose that's what gets all of us punters at it in the beginning. On the Turf there are men for all occasions. There are cultured men, kind men, good men, hooligans and absolute bastards. I've never believed the old adage that on the Turf as under it all men are equal, but you certainly get all sorts. She took a particular shine to Jack Doyle, the bloodstock agent, and kept telling me how sexy he was. I pointed out to her that he was Irish and therefore couldn't be sexy but she would have it. Then she got it all wrong when she reminded me that it was he who originally bought Bruni for seven thousand six hundred pounds. She thought it was good business since that was such a lot of money. I told her it was good business because it was so little money and she began trying to work that one out. I supposed that in a few weeks she'd know it all. Show someone a horserace, wait until they back their first winner and they think they invented the game.

the false messiah

To see a newcomer to racing getting hooked, then
stumbling, then crashing, is like watching a man falling off
the top of a building in slow motion. Take Antonio.
Antonio was the Portuguese barman who served in the
Soho pub I used to frequent. He gave the impression of
being carefree, but really he was manic. His addiction to
matters concerning the Turf began one day when he put
fifty pence on a horse of Scobie Breasley's called Hittite
Glory. The animal trotted up at 100-1 and Antonio got the
idea that he could repeat the performance every day for
the rest of his life. The fact that he didn't know one end of
a horse from the other made things awkward for him and
watching him study the midday *Evening Standard* (as it
then was) was sadly like watching a junkie who can't
remember how a hypodermic's put together.

Anyway, someone told him I knew the odd trainer and
horses, and he started asking me to mark his card for him
every day. As far as Antonio went, looking back on it, it
was already too late to shout a warning. I simply tried to
cushion the inevitable sickening thud by giving him a few
winners on the way down, but I think the results may
have speeded up his descent. I started off by giving him
a couple of good things each day and then astounded
myself by giving him four out of four which he did in a
yankee. The very next day I gave him a nourishing 32-1
double, followed by another winner the day after which
cruised in at 9-1.

I then began to fear for his sanity although I had always
thought he was suspect in the head. In two lousy weeks
only, he suddenly knew it all, and one night I nearly killed
him when he, like a baby trying to walk by himself for the
first time, actually had the nerve to venture an opinion.
'That horse Wollow, he's no good,' he said. So crass was
the remark that I can very nearly savour it now, but at the
time I was tremendously tempted to jump over the
counter and hit him over the head with a bottle of his own
revolting Mateus Rosé. I know a teacher at St Martin's
School of Art who felt much the same when one of his

students told him that Rembrandt couldn't paint, and
there was Antonio, only one and a half flat seasons, a
yankee and a couple of doubles old, telling me that
Wollow was no good. They really make me want to weep,
do newcomers to racing.

I debated whether or not I should intentionally give
Antonio a couple of pigs to back in the hope that it would
put him off and shut him up for good, but even that harsh
measure isn't as easy as it sounds. In the fifties and in the
same pub I used to have a pound bet with a friend every
day in which we'd try to go through the card naming a
horse in every race that would *not* get placed. Time after
time I thought, and we both thought, we'd done it and
then some hack would get its nose in the frame at 20-1.

But if only Antonio's lunacy had stopped there. It
didn't. He acquired an irritating habit of telling me that
the Portuguese discovered the world. Surely, I asked him
the first time he said it, you mean a part of it? No.
Apparently not. Before Mr Ferdinand Magellan's trip there
was nothing. Worse was to come. Antonio then began
falling under the spell of one 'Irish' Des, a man who
claimed that Lester Piggott couldn't ride racehorses. God
preserve us from people like that. Perhaps it's a bit like
what Stevenson said about marriage. Betting on a horse is
a step so grave and decisive that it attracts light-headed,
variable men by its very awfulness. It could even be
simpler. Maybe I just happened to use a pub frequented
by two lunatics.

Impersonating God, giving tips in other words, is a
tricky business. Many tips are simply flushed away. I
sometimes think, when the game is really bad that is, that
the easiest way out would be to get up in the morning,
just shove fifty quid in the loo and then pull the chain.
What fascinates me is the way that people react to
losing tips.

Inured as I am to personal disaster, I have come to
regard losing bets over the past few years as losses of bits
of paper. I don't mean to sound flash by that. I just mean
that I don't expect miracles but don't mind them when
they come to pass. On the other hand, when I do get what
I think is a genuine bit of information, then I feel bound
and obliged to pass it on.

The False Messiah

. . . and then astounded myself by giving him four out of four which he did in a yankee.

I once lumbered a friend of mine, a painter of some repute, with two complete stinkers. He is a fearless gambler and I guessed he must have lost a thousand pounds on the two. I met him on the next Monday morning over coffee and he uttered not a single word of reproach. Lovely and as it should be. I ran across him once in a betting shop. I was moaning because I was down a little 'How's it going?' he asked. 'Awful. I've just lost twenty-five quid and I'm really fed up. How about you?' 'Not so good either,' he replied. 'I've just lost two thousand seven hundred, including the tax.' It was only two-thirty. There had only been two races. (Another painter of my acquaintance used to owe a mad Irish bookmaker so much money that he had to keep painting his portrait for nothing. If you see a show of his, look out for pictures of 'The Pink Man'.)

But others accept losing tips with less equanimity than my painter friend. What I'm getting at is the fact that there are those who mistakenly accept the hunch as gospel. They're not Christians, just punters and I wish to God that they'd get it right. A tip is an opinion. It might be a strong opinion – one stated with some conviction – but it's still just an opinion and if all of them were bang on target then there wouldn't be such things as horse races. Worse than tipping losers to bad losers is tipping winners to idiots and then not backing them yourself.

I was having a shave in a barber's shop in Old Compton Street one Monday morning and the man operating the cut-throat asked me what I fancied. For a moment I couldn't answer him since I'd noticed the most extraordinary thing. Instead of using tissue paper to wipe the razor on after every clean sweep of the chin, he was using betting slips nicked from the local betting shop. Having digested that, I went on to say that a certain horse of Fred Winter's might oblige at a long price. Gastronomic and alcoholic events that followed prevented me from having a wager that afternoon. In the evening, when I read that the horse had won at 12-1, I choked.

At one time in my life, I found myself being followed and I didn't like it. Amost every time I stuck a bet with my unlicensed bookmaker in the local pub the wager was duplicated by a woman called Eva. She had a sort of faith in me that was more dumb than blind. It had started in the spring. I had called round to her flat – it was more of a 'salon' than a flat actually – to discuss the previous day's appalling behaviour and to borrow some money from her. She asked me if there was, by any chance, a particular nag that I fancied that day. I told her that I'd been waiting for a certain hurdler which was running that afternoon and she gave me a tenner to put on for her. That evening, I presented her with a hundred pounds and it was that evening that she got the idea that winning a hundred on a horse was as easy as falling out of a taxi.

In fact, I suspect that she got the idea that winning a hundred was something that could be done on every race, never mind once a day. Well, we had our ups and downs, did Eva and I, and that was the beginning of the best run of luck I'd had for a very long time. We took to having snacks in the Connaught and I went on making inspired guesses and, d'you know, we just couldn't go wrong.

Then came the inevitable period when I couldn't pick anything that even made the frame, never mind won. Well, nearly. But the plucky little woman still followed me. It put me in something of a quandary. In the first place the said Eva, hereinafter referred to as the PLW (for plucky little woman), had the extraordinary idea that money is pieces of paper. In view of that you might think it odd of me to have a conscience about tipping her losers, but it doesn't work like that.

It's something that you just can't help feeling bad about. The nitty gritty of the business is the fact that I can't bear putting money on for someone else even when it's their wretched choice. If you're betting on credit and sticking on for other people you can do your money by the time they send out the cheques or the bills and you've still got to find the readies for your friends. Is that quite clear? I thought it was a terrible sentence. Another thing that's unbearable about getting involved with others is the person who has a go at you when they lose. It's unforgivable in fact. The PLW didn't do that; she was as good as gold, or in her case platinum. What she did do when she lost was bathe me in one of those looks that labradors give you after you've kicked them and which mean, 'I hope you didn't hurt your foot.'

No, what then began troubling my conscience was the fact that my luck turned again and I had two very nourishing touches on horses trained by J. Webber. On both occasions I snuck off round the corner to put the money on, having told the PLW that I wasn't betting that day. I was almost in her boots because I was tipped both animals and the man that gave them to me was furious that I didn't put more on. Megalomania had reared its ugly head. Winning tipsters want to play God a little.

Can you imagine it? That man was actually angry that his tips hadn't made me rich. I can understand it in a way because I can remember feeling slightly irritated with the PLW when I'd given her a winner and she'd said I'm wonderful but hadn't gone on and on saying it. Then, of course, there's superstition and the more you try and despise that the more superstitious you get. On the quiet, I began thinking that the PLW might have been a jinx on me. I knew logically that what she happened to be doing at closing time couldn't possibly affect the performance of a horse in tomorrow's three o'clock at Ripon, but I *felt* it. Mind you, there wasn't much I could do about it. She was hell-bent on throwing pieces of paper at the bookmaking fraternity and if one is doomed to make that kamikaze trip to Carey Street then one might as well have company.

That reminds me. Just about the most honest thing that could ever have been uttered in a bankruptcy court was the classic remark made by the actor Valentine Dyall, radio's 'The Man in Black'. The Recorder asked him, 'To what do you attribute your downfall?' Mr Dyall replied, 'Two-and-a-half-mile handicap hurdles.' What I'd like to know is what about the bloody summer sprint handicaps? Come to that, what about the Bollinger in the Members' Bar, and the novice chases, and the hunter-chasers? It's one hell of a struggle, isn't it?

6

EARLY IN DECEMBER I WENT DOWN TO LAMBOURN TO SEE MY trainer. God, how I've longed to be able to say that. The rich owners of this world may be well used to the phrase, but I get a kick out of being able to use it at last. Let me explain. In a moment of lunacy, I had invested in a part-share in a two-year-old and now here I was being driven by Doug Marks, his usual eccentric self, up to the gallops to watch my filly have a lesson in how to gallop. It was only her third outing and she was accompanied by three three-year-olds. I was quite pleased with myself for naming her Deciduous, since she was by Shiny Tenth out of Elm Leaf, but it seemed I'd given her a name which for some strange reason her trainer had great difficulty in pronouncing.

That morning we decided to settle for his calling her 'your horse'. It suited me and exaggerated that feeling of ownership. It was the first time I'd had a good look at her. She was all chesnut with hardly one white hair, on the small side as would be anyone who wouldn't be two until 1 January. She had a nice intelligent head and seemed quite alert and lively. I watched her do two gallops of approximately three furlongs each and although she was very green she stayed with the three-year-olds, tucked in behind them, with something that looked amazingly like enthusiasm. Perhaps horses actually like galloping, I thought, but it looked like fearfully hard work to me.

Back in the yard I went into Boom Docker's box and had a good look at him. Doug reminded me how well he had run in the Grand National the previous March until being brought down at Becher's the second time around. I watched a video recording of the race and Doug made one of his usual 'funnies'.

'Yes,' he said, 'when I saw him still standing and going well as they passed the stands, I thought to myself, I must start feeding that horse.' Incredible as it may seem, there are a few owners thick enough to take that sort of remark seriously. They'd better stay away from Mr Marks. I remember one Newmarket sales when two Americans approached Doug and asked him if they could have a look at a horse he was going to sell. They were interested in buying him and wanted a good look at him before he went into the sale ring. I walked with them to the box and Doug got the lad to bring him out and walk him around. To the astonishment of the Americans and all standers-by, Doug then got hold of the lad and walked him around.

'A nice little mover,' he said. 'I picked him up for thirty bob the other day in Huddersfield. Got him from a remand school. I know he's a bit plain, but he should make up into quite a nice sort.'

Doug used to send me these ridiculous letters about Deciduous: 'Geoff Baxter rode her out at work this morning. She galloped so well she's bound to win a race.' I couldn't afford to own her. She was syndicated and I just had a leg, but she raced in my name and colours and I never met the other owners.

On Boxing Day I went to Kempton Park. In spite of two great races, the experience was awful and I made my annual resolution never to return. Traditionally, one takes one's hangover to Kempton to give it an airing, but when fifty thousand or so like-minded people are at it, then a day at the races becomes a gigantic and uncomfortable scrum. British Rail, as only they can do it, had started the day off in lunatic style. They'd put on what they laughingly called a 'special' to Kempton and they said it would leave from platform sixteen. A few hundred binoculared fanatics gathered at the end of that platform and waited patiently for twenty minutes and then it was announced that the 'special' would leave from platform five after all. We charged the length of Waterloo and stood champing at that platform for ten minutes until another announcement told us to go back to platform sixteen. The return charge was fairly spectacular. I maimed at least two children and one woman with my briefcase and saw one red setter crumple from a blow on the head from a pair of race glasses. But eventually we got on our 'special' and discovered what was so special about it. It kept stopping. Once on the racecourse I realised that the entire outing was a ghastly mistake. Only at Wembley have I seen so many dreadful people loafing with intent. You could hardly see a horse for the crowd and getting a drink in any of the bars was fifteen minutes hard graft.

That horseracing is largely a matter of opinion was nicely proved in and after the first race. I had a fancy for Bob Turnell's King Neptune and banged a fiver on its nose. The horse made serveral mistakes, but managed to get second, beaten by a couple of lengths. As soon as they passed the post my man on the rails said, 'I thought like you, Jeff, and put forty quid on the bleedin' animal. It wasn't trying a yard, was it? A diabolical liberty, that's what it was.' He continued his slander and I walked back to the grandstand past two men who were discussing the same horse and jockey. 'That Andy Turnell,' one of them was saying. 'he's bloody brilliant. No other jockey could have got within twenty lengths of the winner.' I had to subscribe to the latter view and a lack of moral fibre it was that prevented me from telling my bookmaker that he was talking rubbish. The trouble is, when a bookmaker gives you the best available price or a point over the odds, then you need to keep him sweet. What made him think that the Turnell combination wasn't interested in winning the race was beyond me.

Just before the big race, the King George VI, I realised it was hopeless to try and see the horses in the paddock so I watched and listened on a television set in the trainers' and owners' bar. Would to God I wasn't so easily led. I'd fancied Royal Marshall II all the way from London and then I allowed Dick Pitman's commentary to ruin things. He went on about what a nasty, mean, scraggy individual that horse was and put me right off. My fault, not his. What was so galling though was to hear, after Royal Marshall had won at 16-1, the trainer Tim Forster said the horse was always at his best when he looked like that. I took a really close look at him outside the weighing room when he was being unsaddled and I must say the beast looked as though it had just done two years' solitary in Parkhurst.

Before that race, by the way, Dramatist had won an epic hurdle from Night Nurse and Bird's Nest. It was pleasing to hear from Richard Baerlein, as he handed me a glass of revolting racecourse medium sherry, that he'd napped the winner in the *Guardian*. I was to remember Mr Baerlein a week later. Meanwhile I ended the day at Kempton on a classic note. I like to lose my money scientifically but the holiday spirit put me in the mood for hunches and when I met a bookmaker in the bar just before the last who asked me if I'd lay him Brief Chance I told him yes. The horse hacked up at 9-2 and it must have been the sherry that made me lay him. A couple of points over 9-2 and there would have been an embarrassing scene with me welshing or walking back to London.

Before I staggered off the course, I mentioned to Mr Baerlein that Roger Mortimer had been waxing eloquently to me a couple of weeks before about Fred Rimell's horse Hiram Maxim. Richard said he wasn't sure whether the horse had turned into a pig or whether he'd temporarily lost his form. But the horse stayed fixed in my mind for the next few days. And what a next few days. They ended up with my seeing the New Year in in a ward of the Royal Free Hospital where they told me I might have to be put down.

Anyway, between comas and cold hard-boiled eggs, someone shoved a *Guardian* under my nose and I saw that not only was Hiram Maxim running, but that Richard Baerlein had napped it. His napping it stirred some semblance of confidence in me and I screamed for the telephone trolley to be wheeled to my bedside. Phone calls to Soho were made and Hiram Maxim was backed along with The Dealer and The Bo-Weevil. Hiram Maxim won at 9-1, The Dealer at 2-1 and The

Bo-Weevil at 8-11. The night nurse told me I was looking in tremendously good nick when she came on duty later. I began wondering whether it wouldn't be a good idea to give punting patients in hospitals false results if they lose and then tell them the truth later when they've recovered. Of course, actual winners are the best tonic and it's terribly difficult to take doctors seriously when you're lying there knowing that you're going to collect when you get out. What do you think was whispered into Lazarus's ear?

The Schweppes Gold Trophy at Newbury has now had its name changed but to most people will still be known as 'The Schweppes'. It is run at a time of year when the weather often causes it cancellation. When the snow stays away it is my favourite race of the season, being a sucker for tricky handicaps. That year I fancied Josh Gifford's good horse Tiepolino. He had been gelded in the previous spring and had taken a bit of time to get over it, according to his trainer. He actually sounded slightly puzzled when he told me, but it's an operation that I'm pretty sure would take me more than a year to get over.

The race itself was a terrific contest. I thought my own personal drought was coming to an end for a moment when Tiepolino made a move in the straight, but it wasn't to be. Apart from the excellence of the racing at Newbury that day the company I kept was almost perfect. I met an old Russian gentleman in the bar who'd fled his country in 1917 and who confessed to me that he now made an extremely precarious living out of insurance companies by throwing himself in front of the occasional taxi. His subsequent injuries had made him pretty doddery, but he somehow managed to hobble from course to course when in funds after an accident.

After The Schweppes I took a long hard look at the customers in the grandstand. Much as I love racing I can't help finding regular racegoers, for the most part, quite ridiculous. As usual there were hundreds and hundreds of Lucindas and Ruperts and the thing that always strikes me about them is

The Schweppes

As usual there were hundreds and hundreds of Lucindas and Ruperts . . .

that they are completely out of touch with reality. That's to say they have barely any experience of life beyond the boundaries of Annabel's and Badminton. One wonders what the hell they'd do if they suddenly had to earn a living with their two hands. Apart from that lot there were the lunatic set that I preferred to pass the time of day with like 'Dennis the Chest', 'Jimmy the Spiv' and Lulu Mendoza. God preserve and keep such characters, because the bloody horses won't. One of them told me quite a good story about that cynical ex-jockey Dave Dick. I'd remarked about Dick Pitman's commentaries that I thought he spoiled them by the tremendous effort he made to talk posh. I was then told that when Pitman was riding, Dave Dick said to Fred Winter one day, 'Now that you've taught him to speak like you, why don't you teach him to fucking ride like you?' Cruel on poor Dick Pitman but pithy.

Shortly after The Schweppes I went over to see Deciduous again and the ground was so hard because of the frost that she was simply trotting round the lanes of Lambourn. I'm no expert at judging horses on looks, and when they've got their winter coats it becomes absolutely impossible for me. She looked perky enough and gave me the warm glow of ownership, but she looked horribly like a chesnut-coloured doormat. Doug Marks though thought she was a bit of a cracker and I began rosily looking forward to a touch with her in April or May.

behind closed doors

Lambourn, most famous of all racing villages, I can only describe as an extraordinary sort of alfresco nuthouse. The kernel of the village is the market square, where stable boys booze along with racing pros and fringe types like myself who drop by for the occasional gargle. Drive or stagger for five miles in any direction from here and you come to the outer shell, inhabited by the rich landowners, trainers and suchlike, who behave in much the same lunatic way but on a smarter level.

There's an air of Irish languor about Lambourn. Time is measured by the licensing laws, when in effect – opening hours enjoy a sort of *Dr Who*-style time-lag. Mornings are there for the beauty of the gallops, afternoons for physical resuscitation, and evenings for social and sexual intercourse. Another odd thing about Lambourn is its veneer. You can be sure that strangers, English and foreign alike, who drive through the place think they're passing through what's known as a 'sleepy' English village. After all, there are roses clambering over a few porches and very little noise to disturb the booze-loud glade. But you know what they say about what goes on behind closed doors. Newmarket is tame as a zoo by comparison. In Lambourn they let the animals wander about; in Newmarket they dress them up and take them for walks.

Doug Marks is one of the best-loved inmates of the nuthouse that is Lambourn. A silly oak sign outside his house used to bear the name Lethornes, until his wife Pam got fed up with racing and left him temporarily, and Doug changed the name to Bleak House. He is a crafty punter. He doesn't bet often, but wins whenever he does. He once trained a horse called Singing Bede which broke a course record at Goodwood, steaming in at longish odds. Of course Doug had his money down. He was a good jockey in his day, winning the Thousand Guineas and the Oaks as an apprentice on a filly that would only go for him, Godiva. Then he developed a problem with his spine and had to spend two or three years in hospital. Doug likes to make out he's a bit daft on occasion. Frankie Vaughan is one of his owners and he once danced around the cashpoint outside Marks and Sparks in Newbury singing 'Give Me the Moonlight'.

Then there is Freddie Maxwell, who was probaly unique among trainers in that racing was only the second obsession in his life. The first was croquet. I can remember seeing him screaming blue murder and tearing his hair out because Joe Mercer and Jimmy Lindley told him that they had planted dandelion seeds all over his lawn. They were only teasing, of course. He looked rather like a little Irish gnome, and could talk the hind leg off a donkey. But his achievements were fine by any standards: he helped teach Lester Piggott his trade; trained one of the fastest fillies of all time in Cawston's Pride; and won the Ascot Gold Cup with Precipice Wood. He is still to be found in Lambourn, not in the market square or with his horses, but on the croquet lawn or in the middle of his artichoke and asparagus beds.

As I've mentioned before, the highlight of the Lambourn year is Lurcher Show day, which used to be held on Peter Walwyn's land but has now been relegated to Newbury racecourse. Peter Walwyn was champion trainer twice in the mid-seventies and won the Derby with Grundy. At this time he had two retained jockeys, Pat Eddery and Frank Morby, and the team was invincible wherever they ran their horses, from Bath to Pontefract. Peter is a lovely man, and Bonk, his wife, is one of the nicest people I have met in fifty years. Although I hate parties, I made an exception for the one they used to give on Lurcher Show day. There was always a huge marquee stuffed full of smoked salmon, roast beef, champagne and people. One year I took Tom Baker, the actor, down there with me. I introduced him to Fred Winter. Eddery filled up his glass. Lester Piggott tripped over his feet. Tom said to Peter Walwyn: 'Thank you very, very much for all this. It's the most amazing party I've every been to.' Peter was not at all taken aback: 'Oh yes, well, thank you Tom . . . You know, it's awfully nice to have a few friends pop in for a drink on a Saturday, isn't it?'

The lurchers themselves never held much fascination for me but the people who bring them from miles around to show them and race them are an extraordinary bunch. They are a sort of hotch-potch of Sloane Ranger, gipsy, racing type and farmer. The lurchers – half greyhound and half anything you like – aren't all that prepossessing. I once asked Jimmy Lindley if they were intelligent. He gazed at them racing up the temporary track and said, 'You've got to be pretty daft to chase something that's dead.'

Needless to say it's an excellent day for gambling talk of

all kinds. The engaging Roger Mortimer, a raconteur of some skill, told me an odd story about Richard Baerlein's father. It seems that many years ago the gentleman decided to calculate the chances of life after death. For this purpose he required his family to give him a pile of sandwiches and a Thermos flask of coffee and he then retired to his room for the weekend. On Monday morning he emerged from his study and announced that the chances were 'little better than five to two against'. The matter was closed and never referred to again . . .

7

THE THING THAT DELIGHTS ME MOST ABOUT RACECOURSE CON-MEN is their method of approach. One man at Kempton Park in early March who tried to chat me up had a good new one for openers. 'I'm on the brink of something great,' he said to me. 'Count me out,' I said. I liked that; the use of the words 'brink' and 'great'. It made such a nice change from that stale approach that you should always beware of which is, 'I'll tell you what I'll do with you.' That's a dead give-away, since the word 'do' lets you know straightaway that you're going to be used in some way to their advantage.

Nevertheless, it's sad that the straighter racing gets the fewer characters you see about. I wish I'd seen the dreaded chalk-and-water men at the dogs in the old days. These were a nasty bunch of strong-arm men who wandered in and out of bookmakers' pitches carrying a bucket of water and an old cloth. They offered to wipe the bookmakers' boards after each race for a half-crown. If the offer wasn't accepted the bookmaker would get duffed up.

Apart from the fellow who told me he was on the brink of something great, the crowd at Kempton were an amiable bunch of alfresco boozers. I went to the meeting with a Soho publican called Charlie Stevenson who used to be a tic-tac man up North before he decided to make a profession out of his hobby. In between no less than eight bottles of Bollinger he managed to win seven hundred and fifty pounds, which is a good illustation of keeping your head when all about you are losing their all.

An appalling bit of vanity stopped me from backing the 20-1 winner Don't Hesitate. And I mean sheer vanity. I fancied the horse to beat Pendil in receipt of 31lb, and I approached my man on the rails with the intention of sticking a tenner on it. Now it frequently happens, when I'm transacting my tiny business on the rails, that the bookmakers go in for a bit of banter at my expense. They shout out things like, 'Hey Charlie, guess what Jeff's backed? He must be mad.' On this particular day, thanks to Mr Stevenson's Bollinger, I was taking myself a touch too seriously and I didn't want a load of mickey-taking on the lines of 'The madman's at it again, Bill. He's gone and backed Don't Hesitate.' So, idiot that I am, I switched to Brown Admiral and lost my tenner instead of winning two hundred pounds.

Oh, well. It was still one of the best days' racing I'd had for an age. There was one hell of a tip for the last winner, Mourndyke. As so often happens in this game someone must have done too much talking. I'd heard from an inside source three days previously that it was going to be off and we thought we'd get something in the region of 5-1, with luck maybe 11-2, on the day. To my irritation, when I got to Kempton, the world and his wife seemed to know about Mourndyke. According to *The Sporting Life* betting report in the Monday's edition, 'After isolated offers of 4-1 were quickly taken, Mourndyke was heavily laid from 3-1 to 9-4 (including two bets of £2000 – £800 and £2250 – £1000).' As for the race, Mourndyke drew clear approaching the last flight and won comfortably.

It seems that as time goes by it gets harder and harder to

keep good things dark. You can't imagine a leak from an organisation like the 'Druid Lodge Confederacy' or the 'Netheravon Syndicate' as it was sometimes called in the old days. This was a group of extremely clever and very heavy betting owners that was generally thought to have been founded by Mr A. P. Cunliffe who won the Derby in 1913 with Aboyeur. The brain behind the organisation was probably Captain Wilfred Purefroy, one of the hardest nuts ever seen on the Turf; the other members were Mr J. H. Peard, Captain Frank Forester and Mr E. A. Wigan. Cunliffe died in 1942. He was the poorest of the confederacy and he left one hundred and fifty thousand. When Hackler's Pride won the Cambridgeshire in 1903 and again in 1904, they won something in the region of a quarter of a million.

It's an old adage that no man will commit suicide when he's holding an ante-post voucher. This made it almost certain that I would live at least until Grand National day. In a mad moment in Compton I had struck a twenty-two pound bet: a one pound each-way yankee on the next four big betting races. I had Dramatist at 9-1 for the Champion Hurdle, Border Incident at 16-1 for the Gold Cup, Rhodomantade at 16-1 for the Lincoln and Gay Vulgan at 16-1 for the Grand National. The bookmaker in Compton, Steve Fisher, doubled the bet and came in with me since it wasn't worth his while holding it. So he made it a two pound each-way yankee and put it on with one of the big firms. Without bothering to think about it or work it out I asked him why wasn't it worth his while? He whipped out a pencil and paper, made some rapid calculations and said, 'Well, your share will come to fifty-two thousand if they all oblige.' Needless to say they didn't. None of them.

That year's festival meeting at Cheltenham will be remembered for the death of Lanzarote in the Gold Cup more than for anything else. I had met the horse the year before on my annual spring visit to Fred Winter's yard. We went into Lanzarote's box armed with a packet of Polo mints and –

normally fairly terrified of racehorses – the first thing that struck me about him was what a marvellous nature he had. Amost black in colour, he had looked magnificent and I foolishly thought that Fred's eulogy was more than tinged with sentiment. As a result I tended to underrate the horse until his fatal accident and I don't think I was alone in that. Apart from his Champion Hurdle victories I shall always remember what cracking races he used to run at Kempton Park.

I personally had the worst Cheltenham I've ever experienced. I watched the first two days of it on the most wretched black-and-white television set in Muriel Belcher's Colony Room Club in Dean Street, financially bled to death and spent the rest of the time removing intoxicated publishers and the like from my line of vision. Almost everything I backed to win came second and almost everything I backed each-way came fourth or fifth.

On Thursday I decided to brave the crowds and put my press badge into use. I was driven down to the course by a friend and noted in the car that Meladon and Davy Lad might win. I then did my usual nonsense of changing my mind at the last minute. The only winner I had all day was Rusty Tears in the last, which won at a pretty miserable 7-4. Meanwhile, there was some attactive lunacy in the form of a few hundred drunken Irishmen celebrating St Patrick's Day plus Meladon, Davy Lad and Rusty Tears, and there was some incredible hospitality.

Behind the stands there must have been nothing less than a hundred tents hired for the private parties. My guide to them was Charles Benson, then 'The Scout' on the *Daily Express*, and his knowledge of parties is encyclopaedic. The Piper-Hiedsieck people, who then sponsored the Gold Cup, were giving the stuff away in bucketfuls and at that point I was utterly unaware of the fact that one of my companions was dangerously close to saturation point. It wasn't until we all came to rest in Jake Morley's tent that I could actually see

The Cheltenham Festival Meeting

. . . a remarkable thing happened that I've never seen afflict a drunk before. **Rigor mortis** *actually set in although the patient was far from dead.*

disaster. My friend and companion suddenly keeled over a crate of tonics, came to rest in a horizontal position with his head almost bursting through the canvas of the tent, and then a remarkable thing happened that I've never seen afflict a drunk before. *Rigor mortis* actually set in although the patient was far from dead. It's tremendously difficult to remove someone who's completely rigid, so we had to leave him to make his own natural and somewhat lengthy recovery. Now what I like about racing people is that it's typical of them that they took hardly any notice of the event at all. I mean, imagine that scene at something like the Chelsea Flower Show. There'd be considerable tut-tutting. At Cheltenham they just said, 'What's the matter with him?' 'He's passed out.' 'Really? Have another gin.'

There were further Cheltenham troubles after it was all over. I woke up on the Friday utterly potless and had to suffer the indignity of walking up to Great Portland Street to ask Victor Chandler's henchman Bill Brett for the measly thirteen pounds and twenty pence that they owed me on Rusty Tears. That really was rock bottom.

from bookie to shrink

If you're interested in observing incipient lunacy at close quarters, you should go to a betting shop in Berkshire where most of the customers can only just reach the counter. Most stable lads are compulsive punters and if you worked in this particular shop just about all you'd see of them would be their grubby little hands reaching up with tenners clutched in them. When they're in the chips they really shovel it on. Of course, their downfall in the long run is that they always fall in love with the two they do, and even if they're second-rate selling-platers they still back them and back them. Some boys or girls are lucky

enough to look after champions. I remember meeting the
lad who did Bolkonski when I went up to Newmarket
during the stable lads' strike. All the other lads in the pub
were teasing him mercilessly because although this lad
was on strike, he still heaved himself out of bed at the
crack of dawn and walked to the Heath to watch
Bolkonski work. He told me that the sight of that horse
galloping made the hair on the back of his neck stand up.
It certainly must have stood up when Bolkonski won the
Guineas at 33-1.

But you don't have to work in a racing stable to get
involved with horses and some of my own likes and
dislikes are quite illogical. For some reason or another I
could never get worked up about Grundy, magnificent as
he was. Perhaps it was because I always had quite the
wrong hunch that *this* time he would get beaten and then
I'd be annoyed with myself for having opposed him. In
retrospect, I always think of the gallant Bustino when
I think of that epic race for the King George VI and Queen
Elizabeth Stakes, even though Grundy won. You can get
to almost hate a horse for no good reason. Canisbay, the
1965 Eclipse winner, fell into that category. Not only did
he beat one of my favourite horses, Roan Rocket, but he
was a chesnut and I've got a daft prejudice about
chesnuts. Some know-all was giving me a lecture just
before the race about chesnuts and instead of cocking him
a deaf 'un I stood there mesmerised by this talk about all
chesnuts being 'ungenerous'. Well, some of them are, but
plenty aren't and there are a few descendents of Hyperion
who've got and had got plenty of guts. I fancied Canisbay,
then went off him, then he won at 20-1.

But the love and hate isn't all through the pocket.
I never had a bet on Arkle and I only backed Brigadier
Gerard once at the beginning of his racing career. That
anyone could have ever wanted to see two horses like
those beaten for the sake of a few shillings is beyond me.
But if you really want to see pigs at close quarters you
should spend an afternoon in the betting shop in Frith
Street. I use the place sometimes because it's adjacent to
a few of my haunts, but it's racing's Chamber of Horrors.
The punters therein are mostly Italian and Cypriot and

horseracing to them is a sort of animated roulette. In the
winter they scream for favourites to fall till I'd really like
to put a few of them up on a steeplechaser and send them
round Aintree for three miles. Not far away from that
shop there's the one in Gerrard Street that's used by the
Chinese, and they bet like men possessed. Possessed by
something that makes them very quiet, mind you, but
possessed nevertheless. In yet another betting shop I
know there's a man who's still in love with Harry Wragg.
He must be getting on a bit to have seen Harry win the
1928 Derby on Felstead, but after nearly every race he will
insist on telling anyone present how Felstead and Wragg
would have murdered the entire field.

I back my losers and occasional winners with Victor
Chandler in Great Portland Street. His father, old Victor
Chandler, owned Brighton and Walthamstow dog
stadiums and came into a lot of money after the war. I
first got to know him on the racetrack and one day shortly
after I met him I heard him say to his clerk, Val, as I
approached, 'Good news, boys, here comes the lunch
money.'

I once owed Victor about twenty quid, a fortune to me
then and nothing to him. I'd been avoiding him for weeks.
One day he came into the Members' Bar at Newbury, so
I pretended I'd droppped something on the floor and hid
under the table. After I'd been there about five minutes, a
hand appeared bearing an enormous whisky. Victor's face
followed and met mine: 'Hello, Jeffrey. I should think you
need this pretty badly.'

Percy Thompson, who worked for him, was the biggest
punter in England, bar none. He'd chalk up the prices on
the board, write down the bets, then he'd phone another
bookmaker and have ten grand on. He had one hundred
thousand pounds on Tudor Minstrel to win the Derby,
and he was merely a clerk.

To this day there is a picture of Sterope, the dual
Cambridgeshire winner, in young Victor's office. It's there
because his dad had fifty grand on it at 40-1 in 1948. That's
another story that makes people like me broke.

The last time I was in hospital a couple of years ago
Victor came to visit me, and as he left he said, 'You'll be
needing a couple of bob for buying things like toothpaste

and the newspaper in the morning,' He then shoved a hundred quid under my pillow, which goes to show there are such things as generous bookmakers.

And while on the subject of gambling and hospitals, I was once sent to a very odd establishment in Surrey which is like a punters' research clinic. I lay in bed trembling for a day or two and, when I came to, a nurse told me I'd been raving and saying things like 'I'll take evens.' 'Did I ask for my wife?' I enquired. 'No. But you did ask for The Life.'

In the next bed there was an Irishman who told me that he'd been psychologically unable to work for ten years. 'At one point', he informed me, 'the mention of the word "work" made me feel physically sick.' The psychiatrist in the place was Irish too. On the third day of my confinement, he came along and sat down beside my bed with a great wad of papers, an instrument for measuring blood pressure, a thermometer and a mid-day newspaper. I thought he was going to ask me the story of my life, but not a bit of it. He went straight to he point: 'Do you think Tiernascragh can beat Phaestus?' I had a look at the weights and told him no. 'You really are in a bad way,' he told me, and left to go back Tiernascragh and thus prove I was mad.

When he came back he told me he'd won on the horse but that he'd had a saver on Phaestus just in case I'd happened to know what I was talking about. 'We had a journalist in here once who was so good at tipping we kept him in for five months.'

8

WE NOW CAME TO THE BEGINNING OF THE NEW FLAT SEASON AND I hoped I could start to do a bit better. One lives in hope. I knew it was wise to leave the Lincoln alone, but it was there and so I had to have a bet. The nearer it got to the day the more

The Punters' Research Clinic

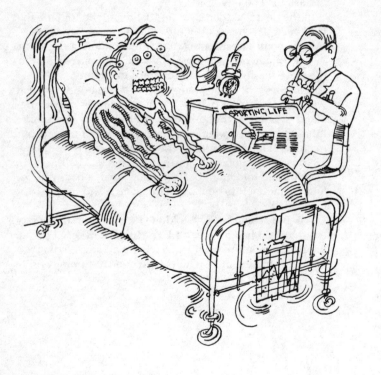

'We had a journalist in here once who was so good at tipping we kept him in for five months.'

I liked the look of Harry Wragg's horse, Fluellen. This one had been reported to have done one hell of a gallop on the Saturday before at Newmarket. He was to be ridden by Pat Eddery and seemed to have an excellent chance. After having great difficulty getting a run, he was eventually beaten a neck into second at 9-1.

Almost the next thing I was aware of was my Grand National party. I had asked a lot of people from the local boozer to come to my flat to watch the race on television. Fifteen of them turned up. The fifteen included three pornographers, one bookmaker, two divorcees, a printer, a journalist, and a ne'er-do-well with his long-suffering wife. I was postive that Red Rum couldn't possibly win for a record-breaking third time and I laid him from here to kingdom come. He won. Luckily, I also took an enormous amount of money on whether Charlotte Brew would finish the course at all. Since I knew the horse that she was riding was inexperienced and hopeless, I felt safe in laying 8-1 against her completing the course. How she got to the twenty-seventh fence still remains something of a mystery to me. But don't be alarmed, I didn't end up winning or anything foolish like that. I took ninety pounds in cash from my guests, went to my local in the evening and lost the lot playing spoof. There is a message there. When you're ahead, don't push it.

I have to report that my local at the time very nearly became out of bounds to me. In a moment of lightheaded foolishness I found myself laying horses in there the next Saturday too. I then worked out it would cost me sixty-six pounds the next time I went in there for a drink, and I couldn't think of many drinks that were worth sixty-six pounds.

I began eyeing the Guineas and soon came to the conclusion that the Two Thousand would surely be won by Tachypous. If not, another suicide attempt. In the One Thousand Guineas I thought I'd probably take a chance with the Newmarket long shot Haco. But aside from the Guineas there was a fearfully important race coming up at Wolverhampton on Monday, 2

May. It was the race I was awaiting with bated, pastis-smelling breath as it was to mark the first racecourse appearance of my filly Deciduous. Geoff Baxter had been continuing to ride her in work and Doug Marks was still writing me boring business letters about the price of oats and hay, but there had been a large number of postscripts to the effect that Deciduous had been galloping really well. Trainers have a tendency to exaggerate the merits of their charges, using phrases like 'He's jumping out of his skin,' and 'He can catch pigeons on the gallops.' My own favourite exaggeration is the one they use after the horse has won a race. Even if it's only got up by a neck the trainer will say, 'He won doing hand-springs.'

I travelled up to Wolverhampton from Euston with an extremely hard nut, physically that is, of a bookmaker who warned me to expect nothing of Deciduous – as if I didn't already know – and during the journey, discussing people who've gone down the drain via the Turf, he came out with what, for me, was the saying of the week. 'Yes,' he said, 'this racing game tames bleedin' tigers.' Quite so. While Haco had been unplaced in the One Thousand, Tachypous had gone down by a length in the Two Thousand Guineas at 12-1, having drifted from sevens.

It was the first time I'd been to Wolverhampton for six years and I'd forgotten just how underrated a track it is. Forget the town, the track is very worthwhile going to if ever you have the bad luck to be in that part of the world. There's a good restaurant in the Members' where you can sit and eat and drink *and* see every yard of how you're losing your money.

As soon as I got to the track I walked over the course to see Deciduous being saddled up. She was walking around the tiny paddock with the others, awaiting their various trainers, and she looked really sweet. There's something very touching about looking at two-year-olds who've never been out. You know they don't really know what its's all about, and when you're personally involved you realise what a hell of a thing it is: you wonder how on earth they must feel when they see that seemingly endless stretch of gallop in front of them from the stalls. They're just big babies. Deciduous looked in very good nick and the only fault you could find was that she needed a bit more time and a bit more muscle on her arse, which is where it counts and where the propulsion comes from.

I'd been pretty sure from the day before that she wasn't going to win, since Doug Marks had written to me from Lambourn warning me that on the evidence of home gallops she didn't like soft going. Her dainty feet got stuck in too far. But if she had won and I hadn't had a penny on her I would have been furious. In the end I made a sort of compromise, not too little and certainly not too much, and had a fiver each way. In the parade ring she certainly wasn't put to shame by any of the other runners. By the time the jockeys walked in to mount the adrenalin was fairly bubbling and here was one of my fantasies at last about to become reality. In fact it was a tremendous let-down. I thought Taffy Thomas would walk up to me, tug his forelock and address me as 'Sir', instead of which he walked over and said, 'Hallo, Jeff. How's it all going then?'

I'd forgotten while I fantasised that I used to get legless some time previously in Taff's local, the White Lion in Newmarket. Anyway, Doug told Thomas, 'Win if you can' and I went into the Ring to place my bet while they cantered down to the start. It came as something of a shock to me when I saw that Deciduous had opened at as little as 4-1 and was third favourite. Did someone know something that the connections didn't? In fact, what the hell was going on? I didn't have to wait long to find out. She started drifting and ended up being returned at 10-1.

From the off I knew she was going to get stuffed since she came out of the stalls very slowly, but it was some consolation to see my colours making some sort of headway as they came to the half-way stage. At the death she finished eighth of the fifteen runners with Thomas sitting pretty quietly on her having not knocked her about. Eighth of fifteen in the 2.15 at Wolverhampton, the Lichfield Maiden Fillies' Stakes, run over five furlongs. Those were the bare facts. But dear oh Lord, what a lot more there is to it when you're personally involved.

Just how much one's life can be affected by racing, and more particularly by the love of a good horse, is illustrated by the career of my friend Conan Nicholas. I first met him over thirty-five years ago in a desolate Soho pub. He told me that he'd first got interested in racing when he was reading *The Times* in the bath and noticed there was a horse called Dante entered for the Derby. Being a bit of a literary bloke, he was delighted that someone should have named a horse after a poet.

Anyway, the idea of Dante obsessed him and he forced his wife to pawn all her belongings so that he could back him at every price down to 100-30 at the off. That did it. He never looked back. Mind you, he very nearly never looked at all. He got a very bad eye infection some time later and refused to see a doctor. His wife told me that he insisted on going to the man who tried to save Dante's eyesight.

For the next few years he had his ups and downs, with possibly more downs than ups, and they affected his health quite badly. He used to nearly have a fit when he backed a loser and the excitement of the opening of the betting shops almost finished him altogether. His next setback was his marriage. He'd decided one day to go to Ascot to see the great Ribot. As he was leaving his flat his wife said, 'Haven't you forgotten something?' 'No,' he said. 'You have,' she replied. 'It's your daughter's birthday party today. What's more important to you, Conan, your daughter or Ribot?' 'Quite frankly, my dear.' he said, 'Ribot.' And he closed the door behind him.

Then he got this bee in his bowler about Fred Winter. We had our biggest win ever on Sky Pink at Cheltenham and from that moment on Conan used to refer to Fred as 'God'. He started to talk like a lunatic all the time. The crunch came with the bad weather. There was no racing for a few weeks at one

Cat Hurdling

It soon became clear that one cat, Kier Hardie, was head and shoulders above the rest.

point and Conan introduced us to what he called 'cat hurdling'.

These events took place along the corridors of his large Battersea flat. The hurdles were made of wooden rods with cloths draped over them. There were four hurdles in all and the cats were induced to jump them (a) by not having been fed for a bit and (b) by placing a saucer of tinned salmon by the front door, which was the finishing post. It soon became clear that one cat, Keir Hardie, was head and shoulders above the rest. Or, if you prefer it, a good eight ounces in front of the other runners.

Conan then had a brilliant idea. He decided to handicap the cats. One Saturday he held an invitation handicap hurdle and tied, with a bit of sticking plaster, an eight-ounce kitchen scale weight on to that animal's back. A film editor from Wimbledon brought along a very fierce tabby and besides the two hometrained runners, Keir Hardie and Nye Bevan, there was also a tabby from Chelsea called Scobie. Like all other mug punters, we thought the film director's animal hadn't come all the way from Wimbledon for the fresh air, and so he was made a redhot favourite at 6-4.

There was tremendous tension in the paddock (the kitchen). After all, we were racing for a prize of twenty cigarettes and a bottle of Chablis. Then they were off. Keir Hardie, from the gate, quite obviously resented the handicapper's judgement and ran sideways like a horse fighting for its head. The tabby went completely mad and Scobie won quite easily, although he flattened the last flight. Much to everyone's embarrassment, we subsequently discovered that the Wimbledon menace had been bunged a pep pill and the film man was warned off.

Somehow the whole business never quite caught on, but Conan never gave up. Even after the weather cleared up he was still at it. I called round one morning and his wife said to me, 'If you're looking for Conan, he's out on the gallops.' I crossed the road to Battersea Park and there he was, walking

about with a cat on a lead. It was Keir Hardie. I said, 'Hallo.'
And Conan simply said, 'Just wait till he gets the sun on his
back.'

ups 'n' downs

The National is one of my best races – after something like
thirty-five of the wretched events I fancy myself
something of an expert at it. As the great day approaches
and every housewife in the country is blindfolding herself
with a duster and poising a finger over the pinsticker's
guide, I find myself thinking that it must be the easiest bet
of all the big handicaps. Merryman II and Nicolaus Silver,
for instance, stood out like sweet cherries. I even backed
Russian Hero, Ayala and Maori Venture, none of which
had much of a shout on paper. But the thing about the
National is that you can always eliminate most of the
horses on one of two grounds: inability to jump and
inability to stay – both vital in the longest major
steeplechase with those old-fashioned Aintree fences
along the way.

The dodgy one to judge is staying power. Russian Hero
– famous simply because it was tipped by what was then
the *Daily Worker* – had never previously won over more
than two and a half miles; Specify was another National
winner that wasn't supposed to have the stamina. The
complicating factor is that a good jockey can persuade a
decent middle-distance horse to stay by getting it to *hack*
round for the first circuit. It was Fred Winter who first
drew my attention to this when he dismounted from one
of his National winners and told the press in the most
disarming way that the first circuit had been sweet as
hunting.

Fred Winter once helped me back a winner at Aintree,
but I never felt very good about this one. He was showing
me his yard at Lambourn and took me round the stable
lads' hostel. Being the middle of the day it was deserted,

exept for a solitary lad lying on his bunk with his head
swathed in bandages. I asked what had happened.
Apparently this was the lad who did Anglo and the brute
had almost brained him with a kick to the skull which
needed thirty-five stitches. I mumbled something feeble
about how sorry I was. Fred looked at it rather differently.
'Actually,' he said as we left the hostel, 'I feel rather
optimistic. It shows Anglo's really on his toes.' I thought
this somewhat callous, but it didn't stop me backing Anglo
come the National six weeks later.

At the time it was a rather horrific and embarrassing
experience. I was very short of readies, unemployed and
living with a paranoid girl of great wealth who quite
rightly thought that everyone was after her money. We
had a party on Grand National day and as I watched
Anglo skip over the last few fences and draw farther and
farther away as though he was having a little canter on the
Lambourn Downs, I could have won an Oscar for my
acting. I knew that if the lady in question tumbled the
fact that I'd just backed a 50-1 winner, then I wouldn't see
much of it since it would be levied as a love tax. But I
managed to hold my head in my hands and moan and
moan and utter phrases like 'stuffed again'. Inwardly
I was jumping over the then unsullied moon.

I have suffered far worse at the Derby. I don't mean
especially from the financial point of view, though I've
bled as much on Epsom Downs as any man; no, it's just
that it's not worth going to the Derby unless things are
absolutely right for you on the day. By this I mean getting
there in good time, getting there in a car (and not on that
travelling luntic asylum known as the Derby Day 'Special'
train) but avoiding the ghastly traffic jams, and cadging an
invitation to someone's box to escape being trampled on
by a hundred thousand twice-a-year punters who don't
know a betting slip from a Chinese laundry ticket. Also,
I refuse to wear a morning suit as I already look daft
enough in my usual clothes to raise laughs from the
bookmakers.

Nijinsky's Derby was one of the worst. A great horse,
but the price wasn't good enough for me, so I hunted
around for a long shot and of course came away with
a fractured pocket. At least it was a lovely day, and

The Derby

In a trance I slowly put cold pieces of cod in my mouth and watched the Rolls Royces glide majestically by.

sunshine always alleviates impecunity. Mill Reef will always stick in my mind because I was absolutely convinced it wouldn't win, and had to run the last mile and a half uphill to the course because of the damned traffic, arriving just in time to see the bugger sail first past the post. I did have the sense to recoup my money by backing him for the Arc de Triomphe that October, the day I lost my job. After the race my Irish trainer friend Mick O'Toole, who had also won, bought the entire stock of Dom Perignon in the paddock bar.

In spite of my interest in – sorry, I mean obsession with racing it wasn't until Charlottown's Derby that I actually clapped eyes on the brutes in the flesh. I did my usual thing. I went down to Epsom with a hundred pounds, a gigantic sum in those days, as they say (and come to that I couldn't half do with another ton now), intending to shove the lot on Charlottown, so impressed had I been with its running in the Lingfield Derby Trial Stakes. I don't need to tell you that I changed my mind five minutes before the off and did my lot. After the last race I remember standing by a fish and chip stall crying. No one noticed since it was pouring with rain. In a trance I slowly put cold pieces of cod in my mouth and watched the Rolls Royce glide majestically by.

I don't believe I've told you yet which are the greatest racehorses of my time, and it's not an opinion I intend to keep to myself. They are Sea Bird II, Ribot and Dancing Brave; then Nijinsky and Mill Reef.

9

THE BIG YORK SPRING MEETING CAME AND WENT. TELEVISION punters who for some reason or other couldn't get to the course, heard a most interesting comment during an inter-race interview when the old master, Harry Wragg, ex-pilot of three Derby winners, was asked about the prospects of his Mecca-

Dante winner Lucky Sovereign staying the Derby distance. He said, 'Any horse will stay if it's settled properly.' Bold words, dogmatic and a tremendous generalisation.

The next Saturday at Newbury I quoted this quote to that genuine expert John Hislop and, slightly to my surprise, he disagreed. 'So how come Hard Ridden won the Derby,' I asked him, 'since he was by Hard Sauce, a seven-furlong horse?' 'Ah,' said Mr Hislop, 'Hard Sauce may have been a seven-furlong horse, but *theoretically* he should have stayed.' We were beginning, or at least he was beginning, to get into the complicated realms of throwbacks. When I mentioned that another Derby winner, the great Sir Ivor, was also thought not to be able to last the Derby distance Hislop again went into a fairly complicated spiel explaining that there again Sir Ivor was so stoutly bred on the dam's side two generations back that the question of his stamina never arose very seriously. It should be remembered that Hislop bred Brigadier Gerard and wrote a fascinating book about it which, along with Andrew Devonshire's *Park Top* and John Oaksey's *Mill Reef*, is amongst the best ever books about an individual horse.

The races at Newbury treated me well on the Friday and the Saturday. I backed three winners on each day, paid for the weekend's expenses and still had a few bob left over. Relkino ran a magnificent race in the Lockinge Stakes and I grabbed the early 5-1 offered about it by Ladbroke's. Not a bad price for a horse that had finished second to Empery in the previous year's Derby. Richard Hannon was kind enough to advise me to have a bet on one of his on which I nicked another 5-1 and Robert McAlpine forced some champagne down my throat, which seemed rather odd ten minutes after one of his foremen on the motorway navvying gang had bought me a bottle of plonk.

On the Sunday I had a cursory glance round Major Dick Hern's yard and had a really good look at those two stars Relkino and Boldboy. Relkino was a magnificent-looking horse, Boldboy too – but a fairly tempermental and dangerous one. There was another Classic prospect lurking in the yard as well and that was the Queen's Oaks hope, Dunfermline. The way she had won at Newmarket last time had convinced me she had one hell of a chance.

Turning to the Derby, I had been expecting some information from France, but all I'd had so far was an eyewitness report from Charles Benson of the gallop that the favourite Blushing Groom had done on the course at Chantilly some ten days previously. 'Not so much impressive,' he said, 'but breathtaking'. But I was still not rowing in with that one. There was a huge doubt on breeding as to whether he would get the trip. I might have changed my mind if Lester Piggott had been engaged to ride him. So what the hell to back?

I would look no further than Durtal for the Oaks with a possible saver on Dunfermline, but the Derby picture was, as usual, getting no clearer as the day drew nearer. Recently I had begun to take notice of The Minstrel and now that Lester was definitely riding you couldn't not take this one into account. And then came the news that Robert Sangster, his owner, had turned down an offer of one million pounds for the horse – well that spoke for itself. One million was a pretty hefty sum of money for a horse *before* it had won the Derby and it meant, in fact, that the animal was worth more then, having not even yet won a race that season, than Grundy was *after* he had won the Derby. This was the beginning of the period which is only now coming to an end when bloodstock prices began leaping out of all proportion to ever more dizzy-making levels. On Blushing Groom, who had at least already shown his paces that year, the Aga Khan had just completed a deal with some Americans that put his value at four million six hundred thousand dollars.

This makes for conjecture as to just how much various men could be syndicated for at stud. I suppose Leonardo da Vinci would have stood for a few bob if he could have gone through with it, but in present day terms some American film star would be the guvnor. But I wander. Though I'd never been so undecided about a big race since I'd taken up giving money to bookmakers, I finally settled for Caporello, The Minstrel and a French horse, Montcontour, in that order.

Meanwhile, day-to-day life on the Turf had been getting me down. At Kempton Park one Friday evening I stood in a rain-lashed freezing gale and did my pieces. It's odd that losing money on a sunbaked afternoon in the middle of the week at a track like Salisbury when you're in good company and holding on to a fortified and ice-cold Pimms can be akin to a positive pleasure. Losing in physical discomfort though is doubly painful.

And following my horse Deciduous was becoming something of a strain. Scratched from a race at Wolverhampton in the last week of May – and me trekking all the way there not realising she'd been withdrawn – and then a few days later at last running really well and getting just touched off. Before the event, at Lingfield, Doug Marks and I could only see one better-looker in the parade ring. Then when she went down to the start, ears pricked and pulling a little, I really thought, for the first time, that she'd get in the frame.

I followed Mr Marks to the rails thinking he might have a pony on her and I was more than a little surprised when he put on a hundred pounds and then, two mintues later, pressed it further. I had a tenner at 6-1 and then climbed on to the stand. I watched the race in a bit of a daze and then when Philip Waldron appeared in my fairly revolting colours – the race card said pink, but they were more like raspberries going off – and he looked as though he'd hit the front at the furlong pole, just for a second I thought we'd won. At the line she was beaten a neck and half a length. A very encouraging run and a fraction unlucky. The next day, in *The Sporting Life*, George Ennor who did their 'close-up' wrote: 'Deciduous, always well there, every chance one furlong out, not much room, ran on.' It was the 'not much room' which was the only bit of bad luck. In fact, in the unsaddling enclosure after, Waldron said that if he'd been second he would have objected. Oh well, that's racing.

It was a pretty expensive day, as it happened. My cynical companion of the afternoon had already persuaded me to buy champagne as soon as we arrived at the course saying, 'If you wait till after your horse has run you might not have anything to celebrate,' and subsequent results did little to improve things.

A far better day's sport in many ways was at Sandown Park a few days earlier. I went with two publicans and my seven-year-old daughter. I was extremely touched halfway through the afternoon when, observing them on their sixth bottle of Bollinger, she remarked, 'Actually, I'm not supposed to have anything to do with people like you.' Not a bad judge already, I thought.

going off course

When not at the races, betting can take on some unusual patterns. I used to bet a lot with a friend who liked to play the amateur bookmaker. Convinced as he was that all punters are as thick as planks, he eventually came unstuck with an architect, a publican and myself. When there was an evening meeting it was quite a pleasant way to wager. We sat outside premises that shall remain nameless and our amateur used to go to the phone for a show. Then we would strike our bets, then he'd telephone for the results and, if we'd won, he'd pay out in readies on the spot. We were fearfully unpopular with his wife who would have liked to have him home for supper at 7.30 pm, but he was not allowed to leave us until after the last race. I had a confrontation with her on this matter and when I explained to her that no man can be led astray who doesn't *want* to be led astray, she poured an Amer Picon citron over my head. It is a slow-drying and sticky substance, and I lived for a few minutes in the hope that

Sandown Park

I went with two publicans and my seven-year-old daughter.

it might turn my hair brown.

Once, when all four of the Saturday's meetings were called off, I found myself in a pub with a bookmaker and nothing whatsoever to bet on. I tried the old one of betting him that the next person to walk through the door would be a man, but he wasn't having any. Oddly enough the next person was a woman, and he would have won. She was accompanied, I recall, by a nice old- fashioned chap who held the door open for her. As a last resort – if you can call Hackney a resort – I had two losing dog bets and then ambled in a desultory and sulky way along Piccadilly. Almost opposite the Ritz, by the way, there used to be and probably still is a rather extraordinary betting shop owned by the William Hill Organisation. It's situated in what must have been once a rather magnificent house.

Décor apart, it's very handy for a punt if you're having tea in the Ritz. The last time I partook of the cucumber sandwich bit there with a lady friend I kept sneaking over the road telling her I was going to the Gents, and coming back with a longer and longer face each time. She evidently thought I had prostate trouble, as opposed to the old fiscal complaint, and I think she was definitely put off me. I suppose the thing is to own up about the betting, but there are girls who would and could never understand that the four-thirty at Sedgefield was more important than them. Wild horses *can* drag you away.

I once leapt out of bed on a Saturday morning shouting a vow to give up backing horses for good and ever. By midday, like an alcoholic twitching for the first hair of the dog, I was looking around for something to bet on. It really is a bloody disease. As bad luck would have it I bumped into my amateur bookmaker friend in Dean Street. We had an idle chat and then, contemplating the weather and gazing at the heavens, I heard my voice say 'What odds will you lay me that it rains before one o'clock?' I was laid two pounds at 2-1 and my request for 20-1 against sleet during the weekend was refused.

Feeling a twinge of guilt at having had a bet at all, but consoling myself that at least I hadn't backed a wretched horse yet, I then had two pounds at 1-2 that the sex of the first customer in the York Minster at opening time would be male. This seemed to me to be something of a racing certainty since I was sure as a man could be that I'd be the first person in the pub. But my luck was really stinking. I was beaten a head by the cleaning lady.

It was after that, while lingering over a refreshing aperitif, that my eye accidentally caught sight of the racing page in *The Times*. Saturday, of course, is the punter's pitfall day. It's sheer folly to try and go through four or five meetings on a Saturday and I felt really pleased about my new resolution to eschew the Turf. Then, glancing at the runners in the Joe Coral Northumberland Plate, it occurred to me that Grey Baron stood one hell of a chance of winning even with his top weight of 10st 1lb. I could of course make him my one final and definitely last bet of all time apart from the obligatory double on Connors and Evert to win their Wimbledon finals. Well, Grey Baron came in third, which made my eyes water a bit, and then I lost a fiver playing my last ever game of spoof.

By now, guilt and remorse, not to mention considerable *angst*, had set in and when at 4 pm, I found myself in an afternoon club staring longingly at a fruit machine, I was damn nigh weeping. Well, a couple of five pence pieces wasn't going to do much harm, was it? The second one I put in produced the jackpot and that totted up to seven pounds fifty. God, fate, luck and love had obviously returned to my side and, as it happened, I realised I was just in time to get on a good thing in the four-twenty at Newcastle. I plunged in heavily. The name of that particular beast still rings in my ears, and how Gold Loom came to be beaten a short head and half a length is something I still haven't quite recovered from.

Let me give you an account of a more typical Saturday's betting away from the course, Champion Stakes day a few years ago to be precise. Take it as a warning. I got out of bed feeling the usual strange mixture of optimism and fear and worked really hard on the afternoon's cards all morning, concentrating to such effect on the Newmarket events that I'd forgotten two recorded deliveries and a final demand by the time I met my bookmaker in Soho. That was at 11.30 am. It was what happened between then and the first race that caused ruination and that was two bottles of a rather astringent white wine. By the time they came under orders for the first, the wit was utterly out. It was five minutes before the Champion Stakes though that I suddenly got a very strong hunch that Rose Bowl was going to get beaten. But by what? Certainly not by the eventual 22-1 winner, Vitiges. I thought Malacate might have a squeak so I put a hurried fiver each way on him. I then read a glowing account of a recent gallop by Konafa and put five pounds on her. Just one more glass of wine before the off and it occurred to me that what with the Bruce Hobbs string being in such good form and his horse Jolly Good having displayed a certain relish for soft going last time out at Lingfield, he must represent really good value at 25-1, so I had a rushed and wildly optimistic each way on that one too as they were going into the stalls.

Half an hour later I had a sudden thought about the Cesarewitch. Grinling Gibbons is about to get stuffed, I said. Furthermore, I mumbled inwardly to myself, it won't be by John Cherry since nothing is going to win this test of stamina humping 9st 13lb on its back even if it is largely in the form of Lester Piggot. I then had a wonderful experience and a rare one. It was a vision. Tug of War was hacking into the final furlong, drawing away from the field and doing hand-springs. So I backed him. A minute later, and just to be on the safe side, I had a saver on Belfalas. It was John Cherry's year.

As you can imagine, funds were now running out. There was only one thing for it – get out of trouble by backing a few jumpers at Kempton Park. Two hours later, sitting under a portrait of a disapproving-looking Mustafa Kemal in a Turkish restaurant, the proprietor approached me with a large, free glass of Raki. It was on the house, he said, because he hated to see anyone look as sad as I did.

10

THE MINSTREL AND DUNFERMLINE DULY WON THE DERBY AND the Oaks respectively. Meanwhile the continuing saga of the wretched Deciduous was beginnning to get on my nerves, get me down and get me into debt. She ran for the third time on 20 June at a Monday evening meeting at Wolverhampton and came in a well beaten fourth. For once I couldn't go to the course and see her, but the next time she sees me, I thought, I hope she has the decency to lower her eyes and blush a little. She actually opened up as the 7-2 favourite before drifting out to 5-1 and that surely must have been a bookmaker's 'come-on'. At the beginning of the day Terry Wogan, then on the breakfast 'show' on Radio 2, had put the block on her by tipping her and, at the same time, had blown my cover on *Private Eye* as Colonel Mad. Then, later in the day, I phoned up Victor Chandler who kindly let me have a credit account for the day and I put twenty quid on her.

It's a fact that I didn't give a hoot about losing twenty pounds, or a very tiny hoot, but what was beginning to drive me mad was this crazy emotional involvemment with Deciduous just because my name appeared in print after hers on the race card and in *The Sporting Life*. When the result of the race came over the blower in the betting shop I was biting my nails and realising how my mother must have felt when I got expelled from school. Before the race, I went in to the 'French' pub for 'just the one' and to pick up a friend to accompany me to the shop and there was a sudden flood of money for Deciduous from various Spanish waiters and people at the bar. You see, that's another thing about having a geegee. Everyone you know is on your side and then when the horse trails in fourth there's a certain amount of lip-curling and boring banter. Even if the horse wins, it's the owner that always carries the penalty.

After the race I retired to another pub to lick my wounds since I couldn't face explanations to a mob of irate Spaniards and, sitting there, having a moan like I'm having now , some twit had the nerve to say, 'Well, just think how Robert Sangster must have felt when Durtal was injured at the start of the Oaks and had to be withdrawn with the race at her mercy.' In answer to that I can only say that whatever Robert Sangster feels it's cushioned by having a few million quid in his current account. Furthermore, when Mr Sangster feels like selling a horse he's at liberty to do so and since his horses are his own or in partnerships with friends he can sell a horse without having nine angry coal-miners coming after him with picks. God alone knew how you got out of a syndicate financially intact if no one wanted to buy your share. Anyway, I now began waiting explanations and excuses from Doug Marks who would, no doubt, have something funny and uplifting to say about the race.

Personally, I began thinking we'd better send her to Chantilly where they get up to so many dodges on the quiet that sometimes I think they could get a donkey to win the Derby. Actually, this is something I'd love to have the time and money to investigate properly. I'm not one of those people who go about saying that racing is all bent, in fact I think it's far straighter than most people do. But I have a shrewd suspicion that French racing is distinctly murky. Which reminds me, by the way, of my favourite French racing joke which is actually true. An Australian jockey who will have to remain nameless got a retainer to ride for a big stable at Chantilly, duly arrived and they found that he couldn't speak a word of French. They got an interpreter to him who said, 'Now the first thing you'll have to learn is a phrase the guvnor might use when he gives you the leg up at Longchamp tomorrow. It's "*Pas aujourd'hui*" and it means not today.'

What a pity that as far as Deciduous was concerned I was beginning to think that it wasn't yesterday, today or tomorrow. And there I will leave the sad subject except to tell

Soho

After the race I retired to another pub to lick my wounds.

you that no, she never did win a race. I later had another syndicated horse. This one was named Colonel Mad after my *Private Eye* column, was by Tower Walk and was trained by James Bethell. I was soon at the receiving end of the usual amount of rubbish. One of those involved with the syndicate used to ring me up and say, 'He galloped very well yesterday. Could possibly win the Two Thousand Guineas.' Such information was not entirely accurate. Colonel Mad was once placed at 25-1 and the height of his achievements was to win a very small event over hurdles at somewhere like Devon and Exeter. Needless to say, I forgot to be there that day and thus avail myself of the quite generous odds about him. He was eventually sold to someone in Switzerland. What anyone in Switzerland saw in an unsuccessful gelding called Colonel Mad is one of those little puzzles that I have never managed to solve.

the luck of the draw

Allow me to refer you to another learned book on gambling *The Psychology of Gambling* edited by Jon Halliday and Peter Fuller. The book is a very serious and disconcerting one and although I've always prided myself on having the ability to 'own up', I realised on reading it that my owning up has always been sheer surface stuff.

For example, I never knew until I read this learned tome that I gambled because I really feel lousy about it and not only want to lose on the nags to punish myself for this blinding practice but, to rub it in further, also want to kill my father. Speaking as an anal retentive who thought that Her Majesty's Dunfermline would be outclassed in the 1977 St. Leger by the likes of Alleged and the French contingent, I always put my punting down to the simple business of asking questions. My main, first and foremost question has always been: 'Is fate, God, luck and love on my side?' The second question has usually been: 'Can I win enough money on such and such a horse to enable me to avoid actual work?'

But I come not to knock Freud, Halliday or Fuller for they are honourable men although I wouldn't mind offering a shade of odds that none of them ever did or ever has had a bet. Heavens above, can you imagine the trouble Freud would have had betting? If, as I believe to be the case, Freud turned up one hour early to catch a train, then can you imagine the trouble he would have had trying to get a bet on the three-thirty while the two-thirty was still being run? Obviously he would have been an obsessive and compulsive ante-post plunger. And, like most obsessive and anally-orientated punters, he would have shown a marked tendency to knock the bookmaker.

What really gets my nanny tote is the clumsy way, or at least inexperienced way, that clever men, intellectuals and academic men get their teeth stuck into vicarious problems. Should you ever have the bad luck or spare time to be asked and then go to a party given by the sort of people who live in Docklands and who write for the *Sunday Times* and then hear the subject of compulsive gambling crop up, you'll find it a racing certainty that some bright spark – usually a feature writer who earns about fifty thousand a year and whose one assignment in the year is to take a trip to the Dordogne to find out how some poof celebrity cooks aubergines – is bound to mention Dostoevsky. There'll then be a lot of wise shakings of the heads and at least two people with After Eight stains on their waistcoats will knowingly murmur : 'Christ yes. Did you read *The Gambler*? Absolutely fantastic.' No one ever seems to have tumbled that what's so bloody despicable about Dostoevsky is that he was a really lousy punter. Not just usually bad, but really awful. You wouldn't have passed the time of day with him in a betting shop.

I don't mean that to be a social worker you need to have been a one-time psychopath brought up in a slum, but I do think that you need to have done a little more than an exam-sitting. (Show me a GP who knows anything about alcoholics who isn't one.) What I'm laboriously and clumsily trying to get at is that you've got to be there to know what it's like to be there. Messrs Halliday and Fuller have written a splendid introduction – nearly half the book in fact, the rest of it consisting of some eight essays – but it's all theory.

I know a historian can write about Waterloo without having fought at it, but I just don't see how two blokes can explain gambling who haven't sweated, panted and drooled over a race card. At the beginning of this admirably unsatisfying and fascinating book that leaves most of the questions unanswered or glibly explained *à la* Freud, there are three quotes. To my amazement one of them begins: 'Sitting here contemplating a load of bills from various bookmakers, I can suddenly remember what made me fall in love with horseracing. There was a boy at school . . . ' The quote is credited to Jeffrey Bernard, 'A Year at the Races', *New Statesman* 1 June 1973. And I think that's where we came in.

God forgive me for ever having been so glib about my Oedipal background but as I've got this far I may as well continue. As a disastrous day's punting at Newmarket never fails to rub in, results depend a little on breeding but a lot more on the luck of the draw. The proof of the pudding is in human beings. Take my own infamous career on the Turf. I was sired by a scenic designer who was himself by a theatrical impressario out of an actresss. My dam was a singer who was by an itinerant pork butcher out of a gypsy.

Another strange example is the case of a Yorkshire-bred friend of mine. He comes from really sound stock being as he is by a dispensing chemist out of a Salvation Army contralto. Full of promise, he came to London at the outbreak of the war, attempted to take the publishing world by storm and now, forty years later, he earns a living writing pornography in the snug of a public house behind what used to be Bourne and Hollingsworth. Taking matters like these into consideration is what the Jockey Club ought to be doing. Where they say the draw has little effect they should double-check and reorganise draining in cases of slightest camber or move the running rails so as to prevent fields splitting into two groups. My Yorkshire friend and I have been running with the group on the stands side for the past forty years and from where I'm

The Psychology of Gambling

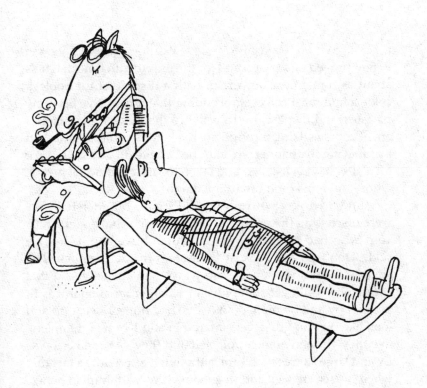

*Speaking as an anal retentive who thought Her Majesty's
Dunfermline would be outclassed in the 1977 St Leger . . .*

standing, you lot on the far side have got a ten length advantage. And we're entering the final furlong.

11

ECLIPSE DAY AT SANDOWN PARK WAS FASCINATING. LESTER Piggot proved once again and for the umpteenth time that he's about as romantic as a woman with a display of the coolest, coldest and most cerebral raceriding that it can have been my pleasure and displeasure to watch. When I say displeasure I am of course talking through my pocket. As usual, I started off by fancying the winner, Artaius, before the off and then went off it after having listened and taken too much notice of people whose opinions didn't matter a damn.

Sound advice came from my old friend Bill Marshall. We were discussing the prospects of the French challenger Arctic Tern who had a terrible reputation for travelling badly. He said, 'Don't go and look at the horses in the paddock. The sight of them doesn't necessarily give you a clue.' I said that surely one could get some idea of whether an animal was fit and happy and he replied, 'No. I've had horses sweat up and look like pigs and they've cantered in and I've had them look like they've been French polished and they've run like cows.' By and large I agree with him, although it's certainly a fact that when horses are well and in good nick, as with human beings it shows in obvious ways. They positively shine, look well-muscled and keen and happy.

Later I managed to get Vincent O'Brien, trainer of the winner, to one side and ask him something that had always intrigued me about racing: horses losing weight and gaining it. O'Brien had always weighed his horses on a weigh-bridge, something that has now become almost common practice among trainers, and he told me that in sheer sweat a horse can lose as much as ten kilos during a race, something like 22 lb. If they eat up well after and recover the poundage, then he had a pretty fair idea that they'd recovered well and had suffered no ill effects from the race. Loose livers with bathroom weighing machines, please take note.

Towards the end of the month, it seemed that I wasn't the only person who thought that Crow would win the King George VI and Queen Elizabeth Diamond Stakes. Bets struck in the Ring just before the off included £5000 – £1000, £9000 – £2000, £18000 – £4000, £12000 – £3000, £4500 – £1000 three times, £3750 – £1000, and £3500 – £1000. The Minstrel won. He must have been one of the bravest horses of all time and yet people went on knocking him on looks, constantly criticising his four white stockings, white blaze and flashy chesnut colouring. You might just as well have said that no one who looked like Olivier in his younger days could have possibly been any great shakes at acting.

The highlight of Glorious Goodwood was the sight of Artaius and Lester following up in the Sussex Stakes, and it took some of the pain out of the previous three weeks when, in the last day, I backed Tumbledownwind at 5-2 and Homeboy who won very easily at 16-1, though of course I didn't have enough on. That weekend was, for me, one of those that you don't get to savour unless you associate with the sort of people your old headmaster would have described as being 'bad hats'. Mine anyway. The paradox about them is that they seemingly drift toward ruination in the most idle way. In actual fact, drifting is an art that requries enormous energy and effort. Come to think of it, it needs a little judgement. It's no good drifting toward Carey Street in bad company. One must laugh along the way. This can be done at Goodwood. I suppose it can be done at some of the dump tracks too, but it's preferable to go down the steepest hill. And there's one thing I'll say about Goodwood, and I'm a dreadful inverted snob about racecourses, and that's that the view standing by the rails on the finishing post is second to none. Shrewd judges, I suppose, back horses that win by such streaks that they don't have to stand on the line. I was driven to Goodwood by a couple of publicans from Soho who are just about the strongest analgesics I've come across. They forced seafood down my throat, a little drink, and then pushed me out into the sunshine to mix with the likes of Edward Underdown – Steward at Newbury and gentleman actor – and Jimmy Lindley who must be about the most articulate jockey it's ever been my pleasure to meet.

The Benson and Hedges Gold Cup and St Leger both produced upsets, with Relkino and Dunfermline beating the two hot-pots of O'Briens, Artaius and Alleged. For me, a couple of the lesser meetings stand out in the memory, like Sandown Park on the day the Variety Club sponsored a race and they had that farce of a marquee they always put up by the paddock and call the 'Celebrity Tent'. Always keen to have a look at a name if only for future dropping, I fiddled myself an invitation into the tent and looked around for a celebrity to stare at. The only people you might have ever heard of in the place were Liz Fraser and John Junkin. The three of us stared at each other for a while, picked out three losers and had a drink while hundreds of people were actualy daft enough to stand around the tent staring at us inside. What on earth is it that makes people want to ogle those they've seen on television? God alone knows. Just as odd to my mind is the fact that thespians really live it whatever they say.

By the end of the day I could just about see the light at the end of the tunnel. I'd been trying to pick winners from a hospital bed for two weeks and that's very tricky. It's particularly difficult studying the form of a race when some wretched student, nervous and with trembling hand, is trying to extract the few drops of blood the bookmakers have been kind enough to leave you. The light at the end of this particular tunnel came in the form of one of Richard Hannon's charges who duly obliged in the last at 5-1.

the guvnor

I once went to Newmarket to interview Lester Piggot for
The *Sunday Times*. He rode two hot-pots for a big trainer
on the gallops that morning and when he got off the
second one he said it was a Derby prospect. On the way
back to his house we came across a loose horse that had
obviously thrown its stable lad on the way home and was
now standing stupidly in the middle of the road. It was
the Derby prospect. I pointed it out to Lester and
suggested we stopped and got hold of it – after all, it could
easily be smashed up by a car. Lester smiled rather
wickedly: 'No, Jeffrey. You never catch hold of a loose
horse. You can spend all bloody day hanging on to it.'
I thought this a charmingly cynical approach.

At the end of the morning I explained that I had to get
back to Newbury for the races. 'You're an idiot,' he told
me succinctly. 'Don't you realise I'm riding there this
afternoon? You can have a lift in my aeroplane.' So we
flew to Newbury in his four-seater with Geoff Wragg and
another trainer. I got out at the races, and said thank you
very much and thought nothing more of it. A week later
I got a bill for thirty-five quid. A little later, a reminder
followed. Incensed by this display of parsimony I told one
of the stalls handlers about it. This same man found
himself loading Lester into the stalls one day soon after.
'Lester' he said, 'that thirty-five quid bill you sent to Jeff –
he's very annoyed about it . . . ' Apparently when the
stalls opened Lester was laughing so much that he almost
fell off.

Lester is astute and funny, but his humour is dry and
abrasive and when teamed up with a brain that fires on all
cylinders it is easily misunderstood. Most of the stories
about his meanness are really about Lester winding people
up, teasing them – like the day he gave Willie Carson a lift
back from York one sweltering August day. Lester told his
chauffeur to pull up at a garage selling ice cream. 'Get
three,' he told the man, who returned shortly and handed
over three cones to Lester. Carson put his hand out for
one, but Lester simply turned to him and said: 'They're

mine, get your own.' This sort of incident, purely an experiment to see how discomfited Carson could look, has been exaggerated to make Lester seem pathologically mean, which he isn't. He's just tight.

I can remember sitting outside a café in Chantilly feeling bored and depressed and anxious about my fast-dwindling expenses – the afternoons are horribly dead even in that lovely place – and who should walk by but Lester. I never thought that worried, taut, serious face would be a cheering sight off a horse but I nearly burst into a couple of verses of 'We'll Meet Again' à la Vera Lynn. But Lester didn't stop to say hello. That might have cost him a glass of red wine.

It's not true either that he never smiles, though it doesn't look as if there'd be room between the crags. I remember a day at Ascot when he landed the King George VI and Queen Elizabeth Diamond Stakes with a brilliant ride on that gutsy horse The Minstrel. He then went on to win the Brown Jack Stakes on the Queen's horse Valuation. In the enclosure afterwards he was talking to the Queen and beaming like the cat that's got the cream. I gather that the Queen had said to him: 'You made it look so easy.' And with an admirable lack of false modesty he had replied: 'Ma'am, it *was* easy.'

Another occasion sticks in the mind. Soon after Vincent O'Brien sacked him, Lester popped up and beat one of O'Brien's best horses by a short head in a thrilling finish. O'Brien was standing miserably in the unsaddling enclosure. Lester walked past him on his way to the scales and gave him a huge grin. 'Will you be needing me again?' were his only words.

As in all departments, Lester Piggot talks a great deal of sense about gambling. I once told him the story of an Italian waiter in Frith Street who put his life's savings on a horse that Lester was riding and which started at 6-5. You don't back horses like that with your life's savings, not unless you're mad, but this man did, and Lester got stuffed that day – beaten by a very small margin – a neck or half a length. The waiter was reduced to hysteria and suddenly began screaming in the betting shop: 'Alla my life I givva my wife good food . . . My children havva the shoes on their feet . . . They eata well, they're clothed, I

The Bad Loser

If you lose your wages, well that's your fault.

paya the rent . . . And now this fucking bastard Piggott,
he kill me, he ruin my life . . . ' In a little while he was
transferred to the Middlesex Hospital in a straight-jacket.
When Lester heard this story, he simply remarked that
people like that are idiots. And he was right. After all, no
one twists your arm to have a bet. If you lose your wages,
well that's your fault.

I don't envy the racing correspondents who, now that
he's a trainer (and naturally a successful one), have to try
and get statements from Lester after one of his horses has
won. He is certainly no orator and tends to reply in short,
sharp, grumpy monosyllables. But for my money he's the
Guvnor of all time. There's a long-standing debate about
who was the greatest, Lester or Gordon Richards. No
contest. After all, Gordon could ride almost anything, but
Lester had many fewer mounts because of his weight
problems. His genius is unique – he's a Jack Dempsey, a
Joe Davis, a Donald Bradman.

12

LATE SEPTEMBER FOUND ME AGAIN AT NEWBURY, THIS TIME FOR
a specific purpose. I could hardly remember – it had been that
long – when I had first started fancying Peter Walwyn's
Formidable for the Mill Reef Stakes. All I do know is that I just
couldn't see it getting beat and was armed with the necessary
amount to back up my judgement to the hilt. As the runners
were cantering down to the start, I spotted Phil Bull
approaching a rails bookmaker. Now Phil Bull, the Halifax
sage, is the ex-schoolmaster who founded *Timeform* and who
knows more about racing than just about anyone in the world.
So I followed him and did a spot of eavesdropping. 'I'll have
two thousand pounds to win Tumbledownwind,' I heard the
great man say. I immediately abandoned my own strong fancy

Formidable and plunged in heavily on the other. Tumble-downwind led until the distance after his usual fast start, but then Formidable was shaken up by Eddery and quickly asserted his superiority. It was Bull that had once described racing as 'the great triviality,' but that was little consolation to me now.

The two days racing at Newbury had been something of a glut of horse manure what with staying in the place for two nights, eating, drinking and socialising there, at night as well as during the day, losing money, then getting some back and then, eventually going down with most flags flying. My own particular flag on this occasion was the white flag of surrender.

Last year, however, my luck changed. I had a yankee up and won over £2,000, a big win for a very small punter. It was the sort of win that hooks a boy on racing, but it occurred to me that since it had taken thirty-five years to arrive at that win punting was indeed a mug's game. I decided to take up making a book among my friends and acquaintances in a very small, fun way. The law didn't see it quite like that and my luck changed again. I got nicked, having been under surveillance by H.M. Customs for three months (always on Saturdays – double time?), no less. It took nine policemen and three customs men in one wagon, and one squad car to arrest me. Little me. I sometimes wonder at just how much public expense. They recovered the vital sum of £31.12p in evaded betting tax and fined me £200 with £50 costs. As the Press at the time more or less said, the law is indeed an ass. Here, never published before, are some of the more ridiculous excerpts from the charge record, *verbatim*.

From the statement of David Bailey, Officer of Customs and Excise:

'On 13th June, 1986 at approximately 14.00 hours I entered the Coach & Horses Public House, Greek Street, London W1. A television set was switched on showing racing from Sandown and York. A man, who I now know to be Jeffrey Bernard said "Does anyone want anything on this?", just as the 3.00 race

The Arrest

It took nine policemen and three Customs men to arrest me.
Little me.

from Sandown was starting . . . [20th June 1986] After the 2.45 race at Newmarket, Jeffrey Bernard handed coins to a woman. A man addressed as Alan on a previous visit to the premises asked Mr Bernard "Did anyone have it?" Mr Bernard pointed to the woman to whom he had just handed the coins. During the build-up to the 3.05 race, the Irish Sweeps Derby, Jeffrey Bernard said to a man, "Dino (or Tino), do you want a bet?"

'I asked a man at the bar for the running number of a horse called Bonhomie. He consulted his newspaper and replied. At this point Mr Bernard said to me, "Do you want a bet?" I handed him two £1 coins and asked for Bonhomie. Two other customers handed Mr Bernard coins and both asked for Bonhomie. Mr Bernard said to a female companion, "I'm fucked if Bonhomie wins." Bonhomie lost and I left the premises at approximately 15.18 hours.'

From the Statement of Paul David Denham, Officer of Customs and Excise:
'On 5th July 1986 at approximately 1320 hours I entered the Coach and Horses. Mr Bernard was sat at the bar. He had the racing page of the *Times* newpaper folded up in front of him on the bar. At 13.45 hours Mr Bailey entered the premises. We sat at the bar next to Mr Bernard and in front of the television . . . Mr Bailey bet £2 on High Plains. I bet £2 on Morgan's Choice . . . My selection Morgan's Choice won the race. Mr Bernard said to me, "I'm glad you won, if High Plains had won I would have been in trouble." He asked me the starting price of my selection. I told him 9-2. Mr Bernard said "So I owe you £11." He gave me £11 and said to customers around him 'That's why they bet with me, because they don't have to pay any tax" . . .

'On 30th August 1986 at approximately 1325 hours I entered the Coach and Horses. There I met Mr Bailey. Mr Bernard was sat at the bar. The television was showing racing from Sandown . . .

'On 20th September 1986 at approximately 1330 hours I entered the Coach and Horses with Mr Bailey. Mr Bernard was sat at the bar. The television was switched on showing racing. Shortly before the first race at 1340 hours Mr Bernard took a folded up racing page from the *Times* newspaper and placed it in front of him on the bar . . . I bet £2 on Irish Passage . . . My selection won at a starting price of 5-1. Mr Bernard pointed to me and said "You had a winner." He handed me a £10 note from his trouser pocket and two £1 coins that were on the bar. The return of the 12 represents no tax deduction . . . Before the start of the 3.00 race at Newbury, Mr Bernard asked me what I thought would win the race. I told him "Print" . . . I then bet £2 on Print . . . My selection, Print, won the race. As soon as the race finished, and before Mr Bernard had paid me, Police and Customs Officers entered the public house at approximately 1505 hours.

From the Record of Interview between myself and A. Cummings at Vine Street Police Station

Cummings Do you pay tax on the bets you take to the government?

Bernard No, well how could I? I'm not a licensed bookmaker.

Cummings Do you think its against the law not to pay tax?

Bernard I do now, as I told Inspector Gardner I always have treated it as a joke between friends. I always take bets from friends not from strangers. Also the governor of the Coach & Horses knows nothing about this, he caught me once and said I'd be barred for life. He knows nothing about today at all.

Cummings Why do the regulars bet with you rather than go to the Mecca around the corner?

Bernard They regard it as fun and are too lazy to walk to the betting shop to desert their drink. It's a joke between us. I think they're fools and they think I'm one.

Cummings Do they bet with you because you don't charge tax?

Bernard No it's just a game. Nobody's that mean, at least my friends aren't.

Cummings I accept it's a bit of fun but don't you think they do it for the tax advantage as well?

Bernard No they don't, it's really as though we're ribbing each other we're taking the piss out of each other in a way.

Cummings How well do you have to know someone before you take bets of them?

Bernard Friends and acquaintances, not strangers. Most of the people are good mates.

Interview temporarily ceased. Doctor to see Mr Bernard (16.57). P.C. Emment and Bernard leave the room.

Bernard and P.C. Emment re-entered the room at 17.04. Interview recommenced . . .

Cummings How well do you have to know someone before you bet with them?

Bernard Friends or acquaintances, never from a stranger.

Cummings Would you be surprised to know you've accepted bets from Customs Officers.

Bernard If I have I must have been pissed at the time, which is quite likely. Have I? Did they win? I hope they got it on expenses if they lost.

Bernard I have never knowingly taken a bet from a stranger put it that way. And if I have I have assumed that they were in the company that I was with in the same way that if you're with a group of people you don't buy them all a drink and exclude one person.

Cummings On one occasion an officer overheard you say "that's why they bet with me, they don't have to pay any tax". Do you still say that that wasn't one of their reasons for betting with you?

Bernard I've only got your word that he said that and you've only got his word.

Cummings Today you mentioned that you were concerned that there were police officers in the pub. Why?

Bernard Because it had been pointed out to me earlier that what I was doing was illegal, by one of the people backing horses with me.

Cummings When was it pointed out to you that it was illegal to accept bets?

Bernard I don't remember exactly a few weeks, well when Norman Balan [*sic*] said that he'd bar me, in the summer about three months ago.

Cummings Did you think at that time that it would be against Customs laws as well?

Bernard That was pointed out to me then.

Cummings What customs law were you told you'd be breaking?

Bernard VAT.

Cummings Is that the tax on the betting in other words?

Bernard Yes betting tax not VAT, betting tax.

Cummings Are you saying that you've known since the middle of the summer that you've been breaking Customs laws on betting tax accepting bets?

Bernard Yes.

Cummings When roughly were you told this?

Bernard June.

Cummings And which Customs law would you be breaking?

Bernard Betting tax, evading Betting tax.

Cummings So is it fair to say that since some time in June that in accepting bets you've known you're evading Betting tax?

Bernard Yes, I've cost the Government about three pounds a week in tax. I'm guilty, I'm not daft. I'm not lying to you or the police.

Cummings Can I just run through the bets you've laid to-day?

Bernard Yes, fifty nine, I think Inspector Gardner said.

Cummings Have you marked all details of bets you've accepted?

Bernard Yes, but not what I've paid out.

Bernard examines the sheet from the Times showing racing.

Cummings The 1.40 at Ayr. Did you take six bets totalling seven pounds?

Bernard Yes.

Bernard 2.10 six pounds, four pounds on the 2.40, twenty pounds on the 2.00 Newbury, twelve pounds 2.30 Newbury, twenty pounds 3.00 Newbury and that's when I got arrested.

Cummings Do you keep a record anywhere of bets you've accepted previous days?

Bernard No, I win or lose and go home.

Cummings No more questions.

Interview terminated at 17.29 hours.

About a month after this coup, the arresting officer, Inspector Gardner, was promoted to Chief Detective Inspector.